About the Author

Having retired from private physiotherapy practice in the UK, Josef, who has been blind since the age of two, gained a BA (Hons) in English Literature. He now enjoys writing, along with frequent visits to family in Botswana. Well known in the small Hertfordshire town of Bishops Stortford, he is a sociable, if occasionally belligerent, character with a friend in every pub.

Dedication

I wish to dedicate this book to all citizens of Botswana, who are known for their friendliness and hospitality.

Josef Lewies

THE SCENT OF RAIN

AUSTIN MACAULEY
PUBLISHERS LTD.

A CIP catalogue record for this title is available from the British Library.

ISBN 978 1 78455 386 9 (Paperback)
ISBN 978 1 78455 388 3 (Hardback)

www.austinmacauley.com

First Published (2015)
Austin Macauley Publishers Ltd.
25 Canada Square
Canary Wharf
London
E14 5LB

Printed and bound in Great Britain

'It should now be our intention to try to retrieve what we can of our past. We should write our own history books to prove that we did have a past and that it was a past that was just as worth writing and learning about as any other. We must do this for the simple reason that a nation without a past is a lost nation and a people without a past is a people without a soul.'

Sir Seretse Khama, First president of Botswana.

'Lefatshe ke kereke yame. Go dira molemo tumelo yame.'

'The world is my church. To do good my religion.'

Inscription to be found on the grave of Sir Seretse Khama, first president of Botswana.

Acknowledgements

My thanks to Pamela Gurton without whose help and encouragement this book would not have been published. I would also like to acknowledge my very special friend, Xgaiga Qhomatca, for his help with the Bushman stories.

My thanks to Gemma Zouhar and Graham Brick who provided the photographs.

And, last, but not least: My thanks to all my family who brought so many memories back after so many years.

Contents

FOREWORD

I was born and raised in Botswana *1, in the district of Ghanzi *2. Ghanzi Town is the capital of the Kalahari *3. In 1969 when I was eighteen, I left the country and these are my recollections of an extraordinary time in my life. Botswana is large, bigger than France, but it has an indigenous population of only two-and-a-half-million. It used to be a British protectorate, gaining independence in 1967. Ruled by a mixed race government it has remained politically and economically stable. It must be one of the most peaceful countries on the African continent. I have a theory about why this should be: If someone should have a political disagreement with another person, it will take so long to find that individual, they would have forgotten what the argument was all about.

The district where I was born consists largely of scrub land, ideal for cattle farming. I was born on just such a farm of white, Afrikaner stock.

When I was two years old, I lost my sight due to meningitis. The thoughts, impressions, atmosphere and ambiences are all mine, so the views and sights I gained were from those around me, not only from my family, but also from the few available friends.

My childhood friend was a Bushman boy of my own age. He didn't speak Afrikaans and I didn't speak Naro, but we had a great friendship and understood one another perfectly. We were of a similar age and we spent countless hours in each other's company, him speaking in his own language and me in mine. We walked and played in the veldt, picked wild berries, followed the plough where we caught and played with the earthworms, we drank milk from the goats, we went in search of the bullfrogs after the rains, we rode on the donkey wagon and we discussed all that mattered in our lives in our formative years.

Since I went back to Botswana, after an absence of 40 years, I met up with him once more and our friendship continued as if it had never been interrupted. It was he who told me all the Bushman tales in this book.

Let me make it clear from the outset that this is a work of fiction, inspired by my childhood memories of the life that surrounded us then. All the humans, the animals of the veldt, the birds and the plant life were subject to the nature of the land. These stories are largely based on imaginings, myths and legends, experiences, recollections and, above all, thoughts and feelings produced by the atmospheres created by the dominant land.

"Creation" is a history of the harsh conditions faced by the early white settlers. In this, the old man could have been my father, or any of the farmers who lived in the region. They had to be totally self-sufficient. Not only did they grow crops and tend their livestock. They also had to learn very quickly how to be engineers, architects and builders, hunters, water diviners and how to perform many other day to day activities. Their level of existence depended on personal and learnt initiatives.

All those who lived in the country depended on cattle farming for their livelihood. The region where I grew up was vast and farms were widespread. Without professional vets and, since animal diseases such as foot-and-mouth frequently appeared amongst the cattle, farmers had to tend the livestock themselves. I have memories of travelling with my father to distant locations. Many were the times we spent a night on the veldt *4, seated around a campfire where we told stories and reminisced. This is reflected in 'Veldt'.

The farm I grew up on was many miles from other farms. For months on end we did not see our neighbours, or even passing travellers. So, when, on very rare occasions, someone should visit or pass, it was treated as a very special event and consequently provoked great excitement. I tried to give a little insight into this in 'Intermission'.

Do ghosts exist? In spite of exhaustive studies, scientists have never been able to prove the existence of the supernatural. But, in my mind, this land with its many open spaces, its sparse population, its loneliness and its atmosphere of ancientness, lends itself to the existence of ghosts, hence the inclusion of 'Ghosts'. 'Berries' tells the story of a young man who is lost and injured, who is cared for by the presence of a young girl. 'Room' is narrated by a ghost, examines the family sleeping quarters and struggles with life.

'Mule' is a series of stories in which I attempt to explain the work ethic on a typical farm. Many of the animals, such as the horses and dogs, were working animals rather than pets. In spite of this, they all had names. I felt that it would be interesting to view the humans through the eyes of the animals.

'Sam', the rooster, takes the reader on a guided tour of the farm-yard. It is his firm belief that humans exist solely for the purpose of acting as servants to the animal life on the farm.

In 'Time' I try to convey the concept of slow moving, almost static, time. Whereas 'Intermission' deals with the solitary existence of farmers, the sameness that had to be endured by all those who are part of this land. Although I say this, don't assume the passage of daily time was in any way either negative, or tedious. In some way, the routine nature of the passage of time on a farm provided a feeling of purpose and security. Time on an African farm was a well-loved, concrete concept. I used to lie awake and listen to the sound of darkness. It was signified by the yelp of a jackal, the barking of wild and domestic dogs, the croaking of crickets and the screeching of night-owls. In some strange way, this raucous behaviour of the night creatures managed to emphasise the silence.

'Legends' are a group of stories, or fables, the type of tales which the folk of Botswana, especially the bushmen *5 would tell their children. These tales, and Bushman dances, serve to explain their culture and beliefs. No doubt some of the stories are used in the same way that we use lullabies or bed-time stories. Because of the importance of the Bushmen and their legends to the Kalahari, I have devoted quite some space to them. There are seven stories; 'Water', 'Cheat', 'Hare', 'Jackal', 'Sun', 'Dove' and 'Rain'.

Whereas 'Legends' tell about the relationship between the different animals of the veldt, the dances describe the intimate relationship that exists between man and animal, as well as the total dependency of man on this relationship.

'Afrikaner's' reflects a most devout tradition. The vast majority of Afrikaner's are very religious and belong to the Dutch Reformed Church, or to its sister churches. 'Funeral' is a rather tongue in cheek view of human nature.

'Lunch' is a description of a typical Afrikaner lunch, on the rare times that a nearby family should visit the farm.

Although the meal takes place at midday, the event lasts for a whole day. The children play games and the adults indulge in endless competitive conversations.

My mother and I routinely listened to a church service on an old valve radio on Sunday mornings. Every three months or so, the district was visited by an itinerant vicar. On these occasions church became a well-attended, event. All would appear in their finery and, usually, the proceedings would be capped by a magnificent lunch.

In Part 2, 'The Present', 'Lodge' is like 'Veldt', written in a different style, to demonstrate the passage of time and change. Finally, since this work is largely concerned with Afrikaner folk, let me give a short explanation as to why and how they landed here.

At the beginning of the 19th century the southern part of South-Africa was annexed by the British, since it was considered to be of great strategic value during the war with France. During the 1830's and '40's, many of the Dutch colonists decided to move north. Many settled in an area, which they called, The Transvaal *7. These folk were known as the Voortrekkers *8. However, in the 1890's, some of the Cape colonists decided to move further north. They crossed the border, first into German South-West Africa, (Namibia), and from here into southern Angola. They were known as the Dorslander's *9. Unfortunately they found the area totally unsuitable for making a living, so many of them moved south, across the border into Botswana. Initially they settled around the Okavango delta *10, at the town of Maun. Once again they were unlucky, many of them died of malaria. This time they moved south, until they reached Ghanzi. Finally, they settled here where the vast majority became cattle farmers. These families have lived here for more than a century. They are a hardy, inventive folk and their hospitality and generosity is unrivalled.

These migrants, together with the indigenous peoples of Botswana, the Bushmen and the Tswanas *11, have the most generous spirit. I salute them all.

****

See the land.

It stretches wide and empty, but its soul is here. A soul which is omnipresent and as vast as the face of the land. The land is harsh and unforgiving to those who do not heed its laws. It is so old that it has lost memory of what it was and where it came from. But, listen! Just listen, and it will tell of those who came to love it, those who have learned to respect it and those it has given grudging respect to. They have not conquered each other. Instead, they have learned to live in total accord. The land is no-one's master, and no creature will ever own it. Listen! Just listen and it will tell all.

Its constant companions are the wind, the occasional rainstorms, the sun, the moon and the stars. They have been together through eternity and they have shaped the land into what it is now. The sun has baked the stones and scorched the earth, the infrequent rains have salved its wounds and the moon and the stars constantly strive to temper its harsh nature with a gentle forbearance.

For the most part the grassy veldt stretches tall and wide, mingled with the shrubs and the now-and-then trees that watch over all like be-crowned guardians. At night the moon and the stars come out to play. They chase the shadows and they enter the minds of the living, persuading all that this is perfect eternity and that nothing will ever matter again as much as this moment.

It was in this land that the old man and his children were born. It was here that he eked out a life for himself and his family. It was here that humanity and earth became lovers.

See the child.

It was in this land that the child saw the first light of day. As far as coming into this world is concerned, it is highly likely that it was an inauspicious birth. Celebrations of any kind would have been muted. The folk who existed here would live in poverty and their daily toil was more important than the mere birth of another child. The land was jealously intolerant of those attentions that were wasted on the living.

Before the child's memories could be fixed, his light faded and since he had no recollection or memory of his first years of life, he had to learn to know the land in different ways. Hence he familiarised himself with his surroundings and taught himself to acknowledge and to accept it with different senses: He listened to the humans, animals and birds, created images for them all and fixed them in his consciousness. He touched the trees, plants, grasses and the earth and gave them colours of his own imagining. He felt the sun and knew its brightness. He listened to the wind: It ruffled his hair, it brushed his skin and it told him of all that was in the atmosphere. Finally, he tasted the air and savoured its substances of dust, rain and clarity. In this way the child and the land touched souls and learned to commune.

See the old man.

He resembles the land in many ways. He is sun-scorched and craggy and he has a constant yearning for the sparse rain. By day he toils ceaselessly in the heat of the sun. By night his dreams are filled with the day's deeds. His labours never end.

When he was young, he was filled with ambitions and hopes for himself and those who depended on him. It is likely that he made many mistakes, but he learnt from his errors and his life and labour skills were honed to suit the land. Not only was he a farmer, by force he became architect, builder and engineer. Gradually, with time, the old man and the land got to know each other. They bonded in mutual harmonious companionship.

He still has his hopes and his ambitions, but now they are tempered. The long term has lost its importance. He is more concerned with the here and now and the immediate future: Will today's milk-yield be good; Will next month's harvest be plentiful; Will the old plough survive another year; Will the rains come early this year; Will the price of beef stay constant; Will his cattle be free from disease this year; Will his family remain healthy?

See the woman.

The ingredients of her existence surround her: The old man, her children and her house. For the old man she provides direction and purpose; the child and his siblings are provided with unconditional affection and conditional instruction and direction; and, the house? Ah. The house. The house with its surrounds of lawns and flowers and fruit trees; the house with

24

its ghosts and many unspoken thoughts. It is from these that she draws inspiration to provide direction and hope for the future of her loved ones.

See the land, see the child, see the old man, see the woman.

THE PAST

1. CREATION

In the beginning the earth was empty and desolate where the house now stands. As far as the eye could see, the veldt stretched brown and barren. Little tufts of brown grass and scattered shrivelled shrubs strained for survival amongst the stones; those stones that were strewn about on the brown earth like misshapen, overbaked loaves of devil's-bread.

And, for the most part, the soul of nature looked down upon this scorched earth and said:

"I have fashioned you thus. I have clothed you in dust so that you may be a manifestation of my power."

And espying the drought-ridden, dust-laden, lack-lustre earth, he said:

"But, now, even I have had sufficient of your suffering. Let there be rain."

From the north, the cloud banks gathered like pile upon pile of bales of white wool and, long before the first drops of rain would baptise the thirsty soil, the scent of rain would fill the air.

Just empty your mind of gross intrusions and listen! Listen! Can you hear it? Can you hear the distant, rich, rolling, wet voice of the thunder? Can you smell the rain?

And, the rain would fall and create a transformation beyond all comprehension. The dry, dwarfish grass and shrubs now stand tall and green. For a while, creatures, great and small materialise from God-knows-where to rejoice in new life. The once-dried salt-pan *12 stands full and inviting, surrounded by hordes of deer and birds in an unrivalled tableau of Eden. Just open your minds and watch! See them all as they joyfully devour their reflections from this pool of clarity!

But, alas, it would not last for long. It was as if this land existed for the sole purpose of allowing stern nature once more to assert itself. And, once done, it would return all to their harsh existence.

Thus was the land when the old man first beheld it. He cast his roving eye upon its barrenness and said:

"I will settle on this land and, with nature's forbearance, I will make it fruitful. A place where future generations might prosper."

He dug two wells: One to the north and one to the south, from which the hidden waters gushed forth. He planted two gardens, one to the north and one to the south. The barren earth became fertile and bore a multitude of fruit.

He took of the brown sands and shaped them into bricks, and the scattered stones, he shaped into even loaves to build a house, which stood proud over all. Nature beheld what he had achieved and he was content.

And, when he had done all this, the woman entered his life. She took charge of him, the house and the gardens. In this land! In this oasis! In this house! It was here that his children breathed their first. Like the old man, their blood was filled with the spirit of Africa and they became one with the land.

****

See the veldt:

It is joined to the land. It is the heart and soul of the land. It stretches between villages, farms and isolated towns for endless mile upon mile. It does not possess any modern road, but it is multitudinously covered by tracks and trails of all kinds.

At first, when it was young, the tracks were only those of animals and men who walked on foot. Now there are the tracks of wheels.

In the beginning, only animals reigned here. The eland *13 and the gemsbok *14 and the springbok *15 ran with all their might and the lion and the cheetah loped and chased with gusto. Far above, the falcon floated and watched disdainfully and believed itself to be the true ruler of all.

Often the veldt is noisy with the chirp and chatter of creatures of all kinds. But, mostly it is as still and quiet as a deep dark soul. To those who know and respect it, it is gently benevolent, but to those who disregard its laws, it is ruthless, wrathful.

See the veldt.

2. VELDT

We reached the village,

Standing drab and dusty in its desolation, on the edge of the desert.

There were no outskirts

With solitary dwellings, standing guard,

Or acting as a beacon for the weary traveller.

At first there was nothing

But the snaking, sleepy, dusty road.

And then, we were in its heart.

The single, sandy street

Stretched lazily between the few houses and shops,

Past the well where the windmill spun in little bursts

In the little gusts of hot wind.

The sun glared brightly
Off the dust-clad buildings with their dust-clad tin roofs.
It was hot -
Too hot for any human activity.

A lone dog crouched -
In the shade by one of the tin shacks,
Staring at six scrawny chickens
Which were grubbing in the sparse grass.
A fleeting thought of chicken-chase crossed its mind,
But was soon scorched away by the midday heat.

Then it was all behind us.

We travelled through the afternoon -
Until we reached the evening and the veldt
Where we prepared ourselves for the magic of the night.

We sat -
Around the camp-fire and stared silently into the red flames,
Which flared with a feeling that could only be the redness of fire,

Cloaked in the peaceful surround which could only be the peace of the veldt.

We listened -

To the silence of the solitary syringa and the dusk -

The dusk which enfolded us in a blanket of serenity.

We looked -

Across years of open space and stunted shrubs and grassland

At the sun which was just about to fall off the edge of the earth.

We spoke -

Of nothing much and yet of everything that mattered,

For that which mattered was not much and our silences said it all.

We thought -

Of the day that was and the many miles we left behind

And we relished with tired anticipation the coming of the night.

We heard -

The noises of the night: At first,

The lone cricket, soon to be joined by its multilegged friends.

And, nearby, in the newly filled lake from the recent rain,

An accompaniment of frogs and toads,

All blending into a symphony of sound

Which was gentle on the ear.

We knew them all.

My father spoke -

With that many-miled-look in his eyes:

'Have I ever told you?'

And he told an unforgettable tale which is now beyond memory,

Because it blended with so many other tales.

In the distance we heard -

The guardians of the night.

The lion roared his disapproval:

'Wife! I am hungry! It is time for you to hunt!'

The jackal gave a mournful cry

And the hyena laughed.

To the east, the wild-dogs yelped

And the leopard, that crusty old gent, grunted them all to silence.

The night came.

With sudden stealth it threw a blanket over all.

The brightly lit, pebble-dashed sky
Winked a salute to all Africa.
The fire also now glowed with the redness
Which could only be the redness of hardwood cinders

And my father spoke.

They all came to listen -
The lion, the jackal, the hyena, the wild-dog and the eland
And with them came the cheetah and the leopard.

The owl settled himself with a wing-sigh in the syringa.
He said nothing, for he was wise
And he knew that silence was the master of wisdom.

We listened.

My father told his many tales -
Of droughts and dust,
Of heat and hunger
And of the plenty that came with the rain,
Like an oasis in the barren years.

He told of those ancients and their gifts of paints and chalk.

Those little ones, who are ancient of spirit even as they take their first breath.

He told of their gods:

The sun and his wife, the moon,

and their children, the stars.

We looked at them and we believed.

He spoke with the lion, the leopard and the eland.

They told of their conflicts, but also of their respect for each other. For, though they were separate, they were bonded by the veldt.

We slept -

Safely wrapped in the magic cloak of the African veldt.

****

See the farm

It is large and it stretches for many miles. Surrounded by other farms which are equally vast. Its large grazing fields are surrounded by steel-wire fences. These serve to keep the cattle from wandering into the wilderness and also to keep wild animals out.

Because of the sizes of the farms, visitors are scarce. Weeks, and sometimes months, go by without guests coming here. Also, farming is a seven day a week necessity and since a journey to a neighbour can take most of one day, visits to other farms have to be planned well in advance. Please, do not misunderstand. The lack of company from the outside world is not considered a hardship. It is just the way it is.

See the house

It stands in the middle of the farm and it has many rooms. It is built from brick and stone and most of its roof is thatched. The thatched areas are cool in the summer heat and warm in winter. The other rooms are roofed with corrugated-iron. It is edged on three sides by pillared verandas. The land here is mainly used for cattle farming and consequently flies are in abundance. The veranda in front of the kitchen is sheltered by fine wire netting to protect all within from the flies.

In front of the kitchen is the yard. Here stand two large mulberry trees where humans, dogs and chickens regularly meet to lounge or chat in the shade. To the left of the house, are two large, shady gum-trees and to the front are the lawns and flower-beds which reach to the foot of the orchard. At the other side of the orchard, stand the dam, the cattle-trough and the well with its windmill companion.

See the farm. See the house.

3. INTERMISSION

It is midday. It is hot. It is quiet. All is still. All is waiting. Waiting for what? No-one knows. No-one really cares. Here, on the edge of the desert, in the middle of the African veldt, time is suspended. Night follows day and rest follows labour.

Within this capsule of suspended time, the old man, the woman and the child, wrap themselves in the endless sky and the sun and the vastness of the African space, until the coming of the dusk, the dark night and the dawn, when it all begins again. With quiet patience, they wait for that which will make a small difference to their lives; that which will provide a measure of meaning and a crumb of excitement in their quiet existence.

The rambling farmhouse, half brick and half stone, half thatched and half corrugated-iron-roofed, stands squat and grey in the African dust. At a short distance to the north of the house, stands the dam, with an inviting, shady orchard of peach, orange, tangerine, grapefruit and pomegranate trees interposed between it and the house.

Next to the dam, the windmill crouches low over the well. At intervals a tired breeze would ruffle the mill's blades, causing it to add its salivaic dribble to the murky contents of the dam.

To the rear of the dam, the cattle-trough stands bone-dry in the sun. In a few hours' time it will be brimming with water and surrounded by the teaming, tramping, shoving, stamping mass of live-stock. But, now it was deserted.

In the orchard, halfway up one of the peach trees, a long, thin, green branch appears to be haphazardly stretched across three other branches, partially concealed by the affluent foliage. A cluster of leaves stirs in the breeze, and touches the tip of the branch. The tree-snake flicks its head aside with an impatient gesture. With a slight agitation along its scaly length, it settles itself once more and becomes motionless. It is waiting.

In the shade, to the left of the house, sits the old man. He is dozing. Gnarled hands folded in his lap. His head is resting against the high-backed chair and his unshaven face is turned slightly sideward. A fly lands on his forehead and crawls down the bridge of his nose. As it reaches the tip of his nose, he raises his hand and waves it lethargically in the general direction of the fly. He does not wake. He is dreaming a slow dream of sun and sand and sowing and, above all, he is dreaming of the all-pervasive scent of rain which would at intervals bring with it an African thunder-storm, to quench the thirst of its drought-ridden earth.

In the yard, in front of the kitchen, a few scrawny chickens are grubbing in the dust. Two tall hunting dogs are lying in the shade of one of the mulberry trees. Rapidly panting, they lie motionless, their tongues lolling from their gaping, salivating mouths.

At a distance of about 200 yards to the right of the house, lies the road. It stretches straight, long, dusty and empty as far as the eye can see. The tall grass along its verges stands thigh-high, its dry blades crackling in the sun, its seed-heads bowed towards the earth in tired submission.

All is still, with the stillness of suspended time. All is waiting.

And, inside the house, the woman and child. She sits in her shaded sanctuary, cool and calm, the colourful cloth of her sewing scattered over her knees. Her fingers move: Pulling, pushing, stabbing the needle in and out, causing pin-pricks of light in the gloomy hall. Her eyes are drawn to the child, slumbering in soft innocence in the big armchair.

All is still.

Then, the air moves. At first, it is more a feeling than a sound, maybe an illusion created by the shimmering heat. But, there it is again; Stronger now. A low, droning sound which buffets the still, summers air. It is the signal for which the day has been waiting.

Little gusts of wind detach themselves from the hot earth and kick-starts a breeze into action. It wraps itself around the wings of the windmill. The little dribble from its outlet is transformed into a high, joyful gush, which arcs glitteringly through the sun before tumbling wetly into the dam. A thin spray rises from the surface of the dam. The smell of water fills the air and, in the pasture beyond, the cattle raise their heads and sniff thirstily.

The droning sound gets louder.

In the peach tree, the snake sticks out a thin tongue and probes the sound. With a scaly rasp, it drops from the branches onto the ground and, with a flash of green, it disappears into who-knows-where.

At first the droning only reaches the old man's dreams. He stirs in his doze. Then, it tugs at his consciousness and he sits up straight. He stands up, stretches and walks round the side of the house where the dogs are now standing with pricked ears. They follow him to the road, along which a blanket of dust is approaching.

Inside the house, the woman lays her sewing aside. The child jumps from the armchair and chatters excitedly. Hand in hand, they move into the sun, at the side of the house where they join the old man and the dogs by the roadside.

The old Ford bakkie *16 comes into view, shaking and shuddering through the potholes of the road. In the front of the truck, they can see the white driver. They recognise him. He is one of the neighbouring farmers. When he sees them, he raises his one hand from the steering-wheel, grins broadly and waves to them.

On the back, perched on two milk-churns, sit an African man and his lady companion. He is dressed in a khaki shirt and trousers and on his black, curly hair; he wears a hat of dust. The lady is clad in a long, brightly coloured dress and both her wrists are encircled by a multitude of copper bangles.

As the truck reaches them, they both wave to the onlookers. As the woman raises her arms, the bangles cascade downwards from her wrists to her elbows with a show of sparkling, coppery splendour in the bright, African sunlight.

Then it was past.

The old man, the woman, the child and the dogs stare after the truck until, after a few minutes, it disappears over the horizon. Only a cloud of dust and the distant sound of its receding engine are left as evidence of its existence.

It was all over.

They turn and with broad smiles, they walk back to the house to prepare themselves for their afternoon's labour.

****

See the ghosts:

These are the ghosts of the land and the veldt. Some are as old as time and others are still young. They have always been here. They are the souls of the departed. There are the souls of ancient warriors, there are the souls of animals who have died here and those that fell prey to hunters of all kinds, there are the souls of travellers lost, or died of disease and there are the souls of those who have passed peacefully in their dwellings. They are mostly benevolent. They are the silent guardians of the land. They would steal into the minds of the sleeping and fill their dreams with hope, to the weary traveller they would give strength and guidance and to the land itself, they give silent mystery and dignity.

There are also the ghosts of the white settlers who died here. Many died of diseases, such as malaria and sleeping sickness. Others died from the dangerous activities essential in order to stay alive.

See the ghosts

4. GHOSTS

I. BERRIES

'What are your plans then, Mister?'

'I will have to make my way back today. I am flying back to Jo'burg tomorrow.'

'It's a shame, man. I think we may get some hunting today. We'll probably go on as far as the great pan. We will turn back tomorrow afternoon.'

He looked at the two Afrikaner hunters across the campfire from him with regret. He was sorry that he could not continue with the hunt.

'Are you sure that you'll manage to get back by yourself? Should the tracker come with you?'

'No. I'll be alright. It is only about 30 miles to the nearest farm and my Uncle's jeep is running well. It is fine, no problem.'

'Well, if you are sure,' said one of the hunters. 'Just travel due south and you will reach one of the farms. If you leave at 9 you should get to Mr Meyer's by about 1 o'clock and he will direct you from there. Another coffee before you set off?'

'No, thanks. I'd better be on my way.'

'Yes. I suppose we should make a move as well. It will be hot soon.'

They poured some water over the dying cinders of the camp-fire and then covered it with sand. The shrubs and grass stood dry and brittle in the August veldt of the Kalahari. The slightest spark was capable of setting off a raging bush-fire.

They shook hands, he climbed into the jeep, started up the engine. One last wave and he was on his way.

****

He had been travelling for about an hour and no more than 10 miles when the accident happened. He was day-dreaming.

A month ago he had arrived to spend some time on his Uncle's farm. Originally, he intended to stay for 2 weeks only, but he had found his visit so enjoyable, he decided to stay for a month. The fact was, he had fallen in love with this country and after a divorce from a childless marriage; he had no reason to return home permanently. His uncle was getting old now and he had invited him to come and manage the farm for him. In return, he was offered a half share in the cattle farm. He needed no persuasion and tomorrow he would go back to England to set his affairs in order. He was looking forward with anticipation to his new start in life, an adventuress future.

It was with this thought that he skirted an anthill and the jeep came to rest in a large pothole with a shattering shudder.

'Oh, Christ. Let's look at the damage,' he thought.

He shut off the engine, got out and walked round the back of the jeep. His heart sank. The left rear wheel was submerged in a 2 feet deep hole and the chassis of the jeep was resting on the ground. The wheel was twisted at a peculiar angle and needed no expert to confirm that the rear axle had snapped.

For a few minutes he stood, surveying the damage, while he pondered his options. The jeep was obviously of no further use to him now. He could walk back to the hunters, but it would take him at least 2 hours and there was no guarantee that he would find the camp again. And, anyway, by the time he reached the camp, they would be long gone. His only other choice was to walk south. Mr. Meyer's farm should be about 20 miles away and if he started now, he should make it in approximately 5 hours time. Well, nothing for it, then. He may as well get on his way.

He reached into the back of the jeep for his water-bag where it nestled between his bed-roll and the cab and he discovered his first mistake of the day. With a sinking heart, he raised the bag in his hands. It was light, dry and empty. He had used the water from the bag the previous evening to fill one of the cooking-pots. He had intended to refill it from the water-tank on the hunter's truck, but it had completely slipped his mind. In frustration, he threw the empty bag into a nearby thorn-bush.

Although only 10 o'clock, the sun was already unrelentingly hot and he dreaded the 5 hour walk without water, but there was nothing he could do about that now. Resignedly, he started walking south.

Then, he realised the second mistake of the day: He left behind him the acrid, but life-sustaining water in the radiator of the jeep.

****

He had been walking for about 5 miles when the second accident occurred. The rabbit hole was partially concealed by a tuft of grass and anyway, by this time he was hot and very thirsty and his mind was not fully concentrated on placing his feet. The act of walking had become mechanical.

He heard the dull snap of the bone inside his boot as his foot wedged in the hole. At first there was no pain. He withdrew his foot and took a step. It was then that the excruciating pain assaulted him and he toppled sideways onto the grass.

Then that he made his third mistake: He removed his boot to inspect the damage to his injured ankle. Immediately, his foot swelled to twice its normal size and he realised that he would in no way be able to replace his boot.

Gingerly he rose to his knees and pushed himself up by his sound limb. Once more he attempted a step and only collapsed in agony.

At a distance of about 30 metres, he noticed a mopane tree. On his hands and knees, he crawled into the meagre shade cast by its bare branches and sat against the trunk, contemplating his now precarious position.

He really had no option, but to wait where he was and hope that some-one would find him.

The hunters would not be back this way for at least two days and he knew that he would not survive that long without water in this heat.

He was about 15 miles from the nearest farm and his only hope was that one of the wandering Bushmen from the farms would find him. It was a slender chance, but he could not think of anything better.

The best thing he could do now was to conserve as much energy as possible. He closed his eyes and, after a while, he drifted off into a feverish doze.

****

He woke with a start and sat up. He was not sure what it was that had disturbed him. He looked at the sun and then at his watch. It was nearly 5 o'clock. Then, he saw the shadow, moving some 50 metres in front of him. He wiped his eyes with his hand to clear his vision. Was he seeing things, or was he still asleep and dreaming? He could have sworn that he had seen a young girl, moving in and out of the bushes. He tried to shout, but he only produced a ragged croak from his parched throat. She must have heard something, because she stepped out from behind a bush and looked straight at him and waved.

She walked towards him and he could see her clearly now. She could have been no more than 13 years old and she was wearing a long, floral dress with matching apron. On her head she wore the light cotton kappie*17 favoured by the Afrikaner women. Her feet were bare. He noticed that she had pulled up the corners of the apron, turning it into a pouch and that she was carrying something in it.

When she reached him, she crouched down and looked at him with a gentle smile on her serene face.

'Who are you?' he croaked.

She did not answer, but just beckoned with her right hand towards her apron. It appeared to be filled with red berries. He reached out his hand and touched them. They were indeed berries. He took some of the fruit and put it in his mouth and chewed. The sweet juice was like a soft balm in his throat. He took a handful and rammed them into his mouth. The red juice was running down his chin, staining his shirt to a deep purple. He ate until they were all gone.

The girl stood up, smoothed out her apron, turned and walked away.

'Wait! Come back! Who are you?'

But, she did not turn. She carried on walking until she was swallowed up by the thorn bushes from which she had materialised.

****

As is usual in winter in Africa, the sun set early, resulting in instant darkness. And, with the dark came the bitter cold. Shivering in the icy night, he realised that the girl was not coming back with help. He also discovered his fourth mistake of the day: He had left his jacket in the jeep.

As time went on, he gradually became aware of the sounds of the veldt around him. He had been in Africa for long enough to recognise most of what he heard. From behind him he heard the call of a jackal; from somewhere in the distance he heard the barking of wild dogs and the hysterical laugh of a hyena; from the bushes near him, came the sound of some animal snuffling. He realised with some desperation that he could not afford to fall asleep.

Fortunately, the human body can only stand so much punishment before the brain would take over and relieve its suffering. After a while, he fell into an uneasy doze, but even in his sleep, he could feel the nightmare bite of the cold and the pain in his leg.

When he woke it was day and the early morning sun was shining in his face. At first he enjoyed the mild warmth which drained the ice from his bones, but within an hour the heat had once more become unbearable. He tried to drag himself to the other side of the tree, where there was more shade, but he was too weak and he abandoned the attempt.

Vaguely, he realised that he was going to die, but he did not care. All he now wished for was relief from his pain and thirst. He closed his eyes and gave himself up to oblivion.

His next conscious thought was of someone touching his face. He opened his eyes. The girl was crouching next to him, just like the previous day, with her apron pouch of berries. He tried to reach out for the fruit, but he was too weak. She took a few berries and placed them gently between his cracked lips. He crunched them between his teeth and choked on the juice. She raised his head and with infinite care, she wiped his face with the corner of her apron. Then, she fed him the rest of the berries in small amounts until her apron was empty.

She stood up and walked away. He tried to call out to her, but all that escaped from his throat was a dry croak.

He looked at the sun and vaguely realised that it was late afternoon. The night would soon be here. And, with this thought came the realisation, uncomplicated and with relief, that he was going to die.

****

The hunters found the jeep and the discarded water-bag and naturally their experience informed them of the situation. They cut his trail and found him just before sunset.

'Is he alive?'

'Yes. Just. But, he has been in the sun for too long.'

One of the hunters splashed some water on the blistered face. A few drops ran between his lips and he coughed. He opened his eyes.

'The girl. Where is the girl?'

'Which girl? There is no girl here.'

The hunter leant down and looked at his stained shirt.

'What is this? It looks like the juice of the red berries.'

'What are you talking about, man?'

The second hunter leant closer to have a look.

'You're right! Now, where under God's sun did he get red berries in winter?'

II. ROOM

I have been here for many years. Try and think of an eternal existence! Just because one's spirit lasts for all time does not mean that one can remember everything in the order that it happened. Things have a tendency to become blurred. I cannot tell you when I first came. It's all so very vague now, but that is the way of things when you are dead.

I remember when the house was first built. In the beginning there were only three rooms: A living-room, kitchen and one bedroom. Then, as the children were born, extra rooms were added. Three more bedrooms and eventually, a bathroom and two verandas, one to the side of the house and one at the front. The large dining room in the middle of the house is where the family and guests gather, for slow talking. I abide with those who dwell here.

I am here all the time. Why do the living believe that we are only around during the times of darkness? Where do they think we go during the day? Ha!

Actually, I will tell you a little secret: Although we exist, no-one can see us. Those who believe that they have seen ghosts have done nothing of the sort! They are merely suffering from mental aberrations. They may be apprehensive of the dark, or it may be that they have overactive imaginations. A trick of the light or a slight movement of an object, stirred by a mild breeze, or maybe a shadow caused by a bird or any creature will be interpreted by some as a ghostly apparition.

If we wanted the living to believe in our existence, why would we wait until the night to show ourselves? Anyway, you believe whatever you like. I am not here to discuss the dead with you. I have to exist with them for eternity and I'm already sick to death of them! I am here to tell you about things that happened here, not just the house, but a particular room in the house and of the child that sleeps here.

Come with me. I want to take you on a little tour. I want to show you something.

It is evening and the light is fading. We enter the house by the door on the front veranda. The house is large, shadowy and pillared; a perfect resting place for ghosts. From here we enter the large dining room and lounge where its old fashioned furniture crouches in the gloom. To the right is a door. Let's enter and observe.

Inside the bedroom: By the door stands a large oak wardrobe. Positioned at such an angle to leave some floor space behind it. This area is used to store fruit. Oranges, tangerines and apples are scattered on the floor where they are allowed to ripen and fill the atmosphere of the room with their sweet, pungent odour.

There are no rugs in the room. The floor is covered with a large piece of linoleum. The walls are similarly bare.

The furniture of the room has been here for so long it has acquired a personality of its own. Next to the wardrobe is a marble-topped wash-stand. On top of this sit an enamel bowl and water jug. The wardrobe looks down on these and they all exist here in totally companionable silence.

An oak timber bed stands opposite the wardrobe, where the man and woman recline on the bed. Next to the bed, by the side of the man, a small side table lingers. On top of this sit a large bible, a book and a torch.

On the far wall, a large window stares into the room. It smiles down on the cot next to it and it winks at the blanket clad child in the cot. He is lying on his back. He is staring blankly at the high ceiling.

On top of the bed the man and the woman recline against large, feather pillows. The man is to the right of the woman.

'Shall I read your story?' asks the man.

'Yes, please!' answers the child.

It is the same story that the child hears every night. He knows it word for word, but his anticipation and excitement are never diminished. It is a story about a very thin boy. The boy is so lean that he is capable of sliding into cracks or crawling under doors. He can go places and have adventures where no-one else can go. The child sits up and the man picks up the book to read.

When the story is finished, the book is replaced on the bedside table. With a sigh of pleasure, the child leans back against his pillow and the man passes the bible to the woman. It is her turn to read aloud:

1. In the beginning God created the heaven and the earth.

2. And the earth was without form, and void; and darkness was upon the face of the deep. And the spirit of God moved upon the face of the waters.

3. And God said, Let there be light: and there was light.

4. And God saw the light, that it was good: and God divided the light from the darkness.

5. And God called the light Day, and the darkness he called Night and the evening and the morning were the first day.

6. And God said, Let there be a firmament in the midst of the waters, and let it divide the waters from the waters.

7. And God made the firmament, and divided the waters which were under the firmament from the waters which were above the firmament: and it was so.

8. And God called the firmament Heaven and the evening and the morning were the second day.

9. And God said: let the waters under the heaven be gathered together unto one place, and let the dry land appear: and it was so.

10. And God called the dry land Earth; and the gathering together of the waters called the Seas: and God saw that it was good.

Quietly, she closes the bible and the man replaces it. He passes the torch to her. These actions have a comforting familiarity, tinged with something else.

'Look this way,' says she. Click! 'Can you see the light?'

'No,' says the child.

'No,' says the woman. Click! 'No,' she sighs. Her disappointment hangs heavy in the fruit-laden air.

And so, the regular nightly ritual is concluded and they all prepare themselves for sleep. They don't seem to know that I am here. I remain quiet and unobtrusive, as the time and place demands. I am not concerned about the child. He is what he is. He has never known any different. But, the woman's grief is constantly, nightly recurrent. Quietly, gently, I soothe and guide her mind towards sleep.

Do not fret for her. As I told you; I have been here for a very long time and I am not likely to go anywhere else. I will take care of them all.

III. PASSENGER

(The Old Man's Tale)

They sit around the camp-fire. The evening meal of potjie-kos *18 mopped up with thick chunks of brown bread and butter is finished. They sit and drink the sweet, black coffee from large enamel mugs. It has been a long day. They have travelled many miles and are pleasantly tired. Their talk is lazy and stilted. It skips lightly between the varied subjects, until it settles on a favourite topic: tales of the dark and ghosts.

The old man speaks:

'Do ghosts exist? Of course they exist. I have met a ghost, not just once, but on a number of occasions. Although, as it happens, for a while I didn't realise that it was a ghost. But, wait, before I tell you about him, you need to know about me...

'I was born here, on a farm in Ghanzi district, in the nineteen thirties. As a young man, before I bought some land and became a farmer, I collected the post for the local farmers from Namibia. You see, there was only a small settlement here, one shop for groceries, hardware and clothes. Apart from the one shop, there was a small medical centre with a single nurse. One qualified doctor was responsible for a massive rural area and visited us once a week. There was a small post office that served mainly as a place where farmers could leave written messages for each other. Post from abroad had to be collected, either from South Africa or from Namibia. The nearest town in South Africa was about 500 miles away. It was half the distance to get the post from Namibia and that was my job.

'I had a young lad who always travelled with me. He was in his teens and left school when he was still very young. He decided very early on that life in the outdoors was more to his taste than education.

'Once a month I would hitch my team of donkeys to the wagon and travel the veldt on barely existent tracks to Gobabis, the nearest town in Namibia. The journey there and back would take approximately fourteen days. On my return, I would sort the post and deliver it to the farmers. This would take another two weeks, or so.

'The journey from the settlement to the small border post would take about four days. I usually reached the border by late afternoon, so I used to stay there for the night and leave early the next morning. After another two days I would reach the post office where I took charge of the post, rested for the night and departed the next day for the return journey.

'Usually the journey there and back was fairly straight forward and uneventful. During the day we would travel at a very steady pace, one of us riding on the wagon and one of us leading the donkeys. When necessary, we would shoot game for our evening meal.

The only time we had to be vigilant was at night. We had to protect the donkeys from lions or leopards. We would make a big fire and take turns to keep watch over the fire and the animals.

'A mile or so inside the border of Namibia, we came to Chapman's River. During the dry season it was a dry river bed with a stream flowing down its centre. We crossed the river at its widest point where the banks were not steep and the river was shallow.

'It was here where I saw him for the first time. I was sitting on the wooden bench at the front of the wagon and the lad was leading the donkeys. We had to take it slow, because, although the riverbanks were not steep, the terrain was very rocky. Slowly we went down the bank and crossed the stream. Just as we reached the top of the far bank, I heard a sound behind me as if someone was settling amongst the bed-rolls. I looked round and saw him sitting there. A young Bushman. He seemed totally at ease and unconcerned. He was not even looking at me. He was staring past me into the distance. Apart from a girdle of animal fur around his loins, he was naked. As far as I could make out, he carried no weapons or any other belongings.

'Where on earth did he come from? I just had no idea. He was not there when we entered the ford, but he was there when we emerged from the river. So, he must have mounted the wagon in the river-bed.

'I knew two Bushman dialects and I addressed him in both. I asked him who he was and where he was going, but he kept silent. He didn't even bother to look at me. He behaved as if he was totally unaware of my existence.

'Oh, well, I thought. He looks harmless enough. He may as well travel with us. You never know. He could be useful in an emergency.'

'At midday we stopped for lunch. The lad saw the Bushman and asked who he was. I told him what had happened and about his mysterious appearance. He walked over and tried to talk to him, but all to no avail. The young Bushman kept absolutely silent. In fact, once again he behaved as if he was totally unaware of our presence. So, we decided just to leave him alone.

'After lunch, the lad sat on the wagon and I led the donkeys. Thus we travelled through the afternoon until we found a place to camp for the evening.

'I halted the donkeys and walked back to the wagon. I looked behind the lad and saw that the Bushman was not there anymore. I asked him when the Bushman had left, but he was as baffled as I was and said that he did not know. He did not pay any attention to him and therefore did not hear him leaving.

'Never mind, I thought. No harm done. And so, we unhitched the donkeys, built and lit the camp-fire, prepared dinner and forgot all about the little man.

'We left early the next day and reached the town by mid-afternoon. We were busy collecting and loading the post and so the presence of the Bushman on the previous day did not cross our minds.

'The next day we made our return journey which was totally uneventful. We reached Ghanzi town some six days later and after a night's rest, we sorted the post and went on our way to deliver it to the different farms. It was all very routine stuff and so the time passed until we had to make the journey once more.

'Nothing happened until we reached the little river in Namibia. We crossed it and as we reached the far bank, the lad looked back and stopped. He walked back to where I was perched and told me to look behind me. I turned round and gasped with surprise. The Bushman was sitting there, exactly as before. I spoke to him, but again he ignored me completely. Once more it was as if he was totally unaware of our presence. As before, he just sat and stared into the distance.

'I told the lad just to leave him alone. I did not think that he would do us any harm. So we continued on our journey, but as on the previous occasion, when we reached our evening camp site, the little man was gone.

'As previously, we forgot all about him. We collected the post and made our way back home.

'For the next year or so, events repeated themselves: The little man would join us at the river and leave us by evening. We took him for granted. I believed that he was working in the area of the river and that he was just hitching a lift home. Anyway, he seemed harmless and consequently we never bothered to ask any questions about him.

'And then, as suddenly as he appeared, he disappeared. One day, we crossed the river as usual. I was so used to the little man joining us and therefore I did not look for him. I don't know why I did it, but after a few miles, I looked back and saw that the space where he normally sat was empty. Not only was I surprised by this, but I was also filled with a feeling of sadness. It was as if a dear, expected friend had deserted me and was not there to greet me.

'On this occasion we did not forget him. During the next two days we constantly wondered about him. I decided to make some enquiries when we reached the town.

'So, when we had collected and loaded the post, I approached the post master and took him aside where I told him all about the little man. He listened patiently to my story, lit his pipe and said:

"You know. I can't be totally sure, but I think I know who he is. I don't really want to believe, but, you see, now that you have described the little man and the circumstances of your meeting with him, I suspect that I have no choice in the matter."

'Then, tell me. Who do you think he is?'

"Let me tell you a little story," said the post master. "Just outside the town here lived a farmer, a Mr van Zyl. Not a very nice man. He was not good with his farm workers. In fact, it was said that he treated them like slaves, that he was prone to punish them with severe beatings for no good reason.

"Five years ago, we had some extraordinary heavy rains in this area and the river near the border was unusually high. Van Zyl had to go on business to Botswana and he took two of his Bushman workers with him. He decided to make the journey by ox-wagon. When he reached the river, he was surprised at the strength and depth of the stream and he was not sure that the oxen would cope. So, van Zyl told one of his workers to go into the ford to test the strength of the current. The lad refused and, according to the other Bushman, van Zyl gave him a severe beating. Still the little man refused at which van Zyl flew into a rage, picked him up and flung him into the current. No need to say, the water was too deep and the current too strong for him. He was swept downstream and never seen again.

"A few months after that, van Zyl also met his end. He was discovered drowned in his well. No-one knows how it happened, but there were rumours that he was pushed. There were also stories about sightings on the farm of the young Bushman that van Zyl had drowned.

"So," continued the post master. "I have never believed in ghosts, but, reluctantly, I have to wonder, maybe you did meet van Zyl's victim."

The old man fills his pipe, lights it and speaks again:

'I was very interested in this story and I made some further enquiries in the area. It appeared that there had been many sightings of our young man, both by travellers at the river-crossing and on the farm.'

He stretches and yawns:

'I have not travelled that way for many years now. There's a bridge over the river now. I don't know if he is still there or not, but I would like to believe that he's still hitching lifts on the back of trucks.'

****

See me. I am the mule.

I am neither horse, nor donkey. Physically, I am squat and ugly. I am also dumb. Because of all this, I am neither proud, nor vain. But, I am not stupid.

I am also very compliant and I tolerate man and beast on equal terms. Because I appear so insignificant, no beast considers me as a threat and the humans are usually kind to their beasts. Let's face it. They really do not have much of a choice in the matter. We are all working animals and there would be no profit in abusing us. We are interdependent, as

61

the humans feed and groom us; they in turn need us for our strength to carry them and their loads. I am also of the opinion that animals and humans are friends at heart.

I would like to tell you about all the things that happened to me on the farm and some of the things the humans got up to. I live on the farm with two horses. I have known them since I was a foal. They are my friends. This is my story.

See me. I am the mule.

5. MULE

I. BIRTH

It is that hour, just after sunset, but just before dark when the day is running down and its clammers are gradually ceasing, when the night is just about to begin and its own special noises are preparing themselves for their onslaught on the waiting world. That time when the soul is still and the mind is at peace and the body is tired, but at rest from its daily toil. A lone cicada tries to prolong the day by beating out its croaky song with its raspy wings on scaly legs, but finally even it has to succumb to the hour. It stutters and falls silent and all that can be heard now is the faint rattle of leaves in the old marula tree, stirred by a hesitating little breeze.

The red-brick house stands quiet and tranquil in the dusk. The corrugated iron roof crackles as it contracts in the cooler air of the evening. It is also settling down for the night. Even the interminable flies, which plague all cattle farms, seemed to have given up their harassment for the day and the protective screen door to the kitchen is wedged wide to allow some cooler air to circulate through the house.

Some 50 metres to the left of the house, is a little paddock. Here, in the gloom, three animals can be seen: A donkey, a mare and a little stallion foal, the off-spring of the horse. The donkey and the horse have their heads bowed towards the sparse grass, while the foal is tottering on unsteady legs, nuzzling at its mother for milk. The donkey and the mare have their heads close together as if in deep conversation. Whilst the horse is pulling at the shreds of grass and munching with contentment, there is a despondent look about the donkey. At frequent intervals, she gives little grunts as if she is in pain and there is a listless look about her. She is evidently in distress.

The squeak of a gate breaks the silence and a middle-aged African man enters the farm yard in front of the house. He is tall and very dark and although he is carrying a bucket of fresh milk in each hand, his movements are graceful and his step is light. He places the two buckets on the step in front of the screen-door and veers off to the left. He makes his way towards the paddock. He gives a cursory glance at the horse and her foal and then his eyes steady on the donkey. He stares at her intently for a few minutes and a little frown of concern crosses his face. He ducks between two strands of the steel-wire fence which surround the paddock and makes his way to the donkey. He runs his hands down her sides and with gentle, but firm fingers, he prods her stomach. The donkey stands quietly while the examination is taking place. The man grunts as if he was satisfied with his findings, turns away, climbs back through the fence and makes his way back to the house. When he reaches the house, he picks up the two buckets of milk, stamps his feet to remove most of the dust from his shoes and to announce himself to those inside and enters the kitchen.

An African woman is wiping a cup on a cloth. She reaches up and places it with the other crockery in the old kitchen dresser. She glowers up at the man:

'Ezra! You are late! Where have you been all this time? I hope you have cleaned your shoes before you came in. This is not any old hut which you can treat like a pigsty. I have spent all day on my knees polishing this floor. Have you brought me some milk?'

'Rachael! You have a sharp tongue on you! I have been to see Lily. She is having trouble. I fear for her and her unborn child. Of course I have brought the milk. Where do you want it?'

'Put it there on the table. You better go and see Master Dannie.'

He places the two buckets of milk on the table and leaves the kitchen.

On a wide strip of lawn, in front of the house, dotted with colourful flowers, we find the Le Roux family, sitting on rugs: Mr Dannie Le Roux, his wife, Maria, 14 year old Louis and 12 year old Bess. Mr Le Roux is smoking his pipe, Mrs Le Roux is slicing runner-beans into an enamel bowl and the children are idly lounging. They are talking restfully and quietly about all those things which are of little relevance to other people, but which are absolutely central to their own lives and the farming community in the area. Their talk is about fencing and digging, ploughing and hoeing, planting and harvesting, cutting and splicing, moulding and building, grazing and milk yields, the sale price of cream and the sale price of beef. They talk about neighbours and friends, the increased cost of living and the increased cost of labour, of sand and dust, of rain and wind, of night and day, of life and death. The children had recently returned from a school far away for their summer break and their talk is about school and holidays.

Ezra appears from round the corner of the house and approaches the group on the rugs. When he reaches them, he sinks down on his haunches.

Dannie Le Roux fills his pipe: 'Evening, Ezra. You seem worried. What's the trouble?'

'It is Lily, Sir. She is having big problems with her unborn foal. They have been fighting each other all day.'

Mr Le Roux strikes a match and lights his pipe.

'Let's go and have a look at her.'

The boy rises to his feet. 'May I come too?'

Mr Le Roux smiles: 'Yes. Come along. It is time you learned about these things.'

The three of them disappear around the corner and make their way towards the paddock.

In the paddock, the donkey groans deep in her throat: 'Oh, Bella. This child inside me is giving me a lot of pain.'

'The mare looks at her and says kindly: 'Yes. But, it will soon be over.'

'I know. But, I will not be here to tend to him. Will you look after him for me?'

The horse pulls up a tuft of grass and chews. She is not eating because she is hungry, but because the grass is there and it helps her to think. 'Yes. I will do that. His father is also the father of my little one and they shall be reared as brothers. Look! Here comes Master James, Ezra and little Louis. As far as humans go, they are very kind and they will look after you.'

The three men enter the paddock and Danny Le Roux examines the donkey. "The foal is large. That is probably because the father was a horse. It has also turned inside the mother. She's going to need help. It will probably kill her. Louis. Go back to the house and fetch a lantern. It is beginning to get dark.'

Louis runs off and returns a few minutes later with the light.

An hour later, the little mule child is born. Ezra picks him up and carries him round to the front of his mother. The donkey raises her head, licks the face of her child and dies.

II. FOAL

I do not remember much about the first few days of my life. I was born in the summer, a very long time ago. My father was a horse called Diamond and my mother was a donkey called Lily. So, the humans combined the names of my mother and my father and they called me, Dilly. My half-brother is called Nelson. Diamond, our father, was sold to a neighbour who was in need of a good stallion, a few weeks before my birth.

Nelson's mother Bella was a proud mare. She was sort of mother to both of us, since mother died when I was born. Bella and Diamond are also long dead now.

I am happy to say that Nelson is still alive, we are quite old now. We grew up together, worked together and lived together, and very kindly, the humans decided to give us shelter in our old age in our own little paddock. Here we spend our days in companionable solitude. Most of the time we just graze on the short grass, or talk about days gone by and all the things that happened on the farm.

As I said, I do not remember too much about the first few days of my life. I have a vague memory of seeing my mother's face in real life once, but I can't be sure. However, I do know what she looked like. You see, she often appears to me in the quiet of my dreams. This is when I talk to her and tell her about everything on the farm and of all the things that have happened to me.

She was a lovely lady. Her colouring was a deep brown, except for her broad forehead which sported a triangle of white, shaggy hair. I look a lot like my mother, except that I am a lot larger and sturdier. That is because my father was a horse.

As soon as I was born, I was taken into the farmhouse where I was looked after until such time as I was strong enough to face the outside world. This in itself was a very unusual occurrence. Not a lot of animals had the privilege of entering Mrs Le Roux's domain. She was exceedingly proud of her house. Even Mr Le Roux and Ezra used to get a good telling off from Mrs Le Roux and Rachael if they should come into the kitchen with their muddy boots on.

During the time that I lived in the kitchen, a goat kid and a little calf were brought in to join me. You see, we were all born during the time of the great drought and there was not a lot of food and water around for the animals. So, the lamb and the calves' mothers' just didn't have enough milk to feed them.

Ah! We had a lovely time in the kitchen! We were fed warm milk from bottles with rubber teats. Everybody made a terrible fuss of us, especially Louis and Bess.

The lamb was called, Sarah and the calf was called Gertie. We slept in large cardboard boxes filled with lovely, warm straw and became very good friends. This friendship lasted long after we left the house.

Our wonderful time in the kitchen was not to last for very long though. Something rather unfortunate occurred to bring about our expulsion. You see, Sarah did not know that she was doing anything wrong. She just did something which all animals regularly do, because they have to do it, otherwise they become very uncomfortable. The only problem was that she did it in front of the stove and when Mr Le Roux came into the kitchen one morning to make the early morning coffee, he stepped in it, because he didn't see it. As he walked backwards and forwards across the kitchen collecting cups, saucers and spoons, he spread Sarah's little parcel all over the floor. Mrs Le Roux was not happy at all!

'That is it! These animals will have to go! I will not allow you and the animals to turn this house into a pigsty.'

Mr Le Roux looked around and announced rather vaguely that he could see no pigs in the vicinity, a comment which served no better purpose than to earn him a wet clout behind the head with a mop.

We were promptly removed from the house. I went back to Bella and Nelson. Sarah and Gertie went back to their mothers.

Life on the farm had now really begun. Although we now lived outside, the humans still took special care of me and Nelson. This was because Bella did not have enough milk for both of us. So, for a while Ezra and Louis brought us extra milk from the house until we began to eat solid food, we got extra rations of hay. However we were both strong and healthy animals and after a number of months, we were fully grown and we could fend for ourselves.

Nelson and I became inseparable friends, a fact which initially caused a few problems with the humans. Let me explain.

There were many different types of animals on the farm: Chickens, horses, dogs, donkeys, sheep, pigs and cattle. Each group of animals had their own specific duties to perform. The chickens laid eggs, the cows provided milk, the donkeys pulled the plough and the wagon, the dogs were used for hunting and the horses were used to carry the humans around the farm. At first I didn't know what the pigs and the sheep did. I was only aware that, when they reached a certain age, they would leave the farm, never to return again. This also happened to some of the cattle. It was not until a lot later that I found out where they went, but that is another part of my tale.

The farm on which we lived, like all other farms in this part of Africa, was very large and there were very few roads. There were also many steel-wire fences on our farm, which served two purposes: Firstly, they stopped the animals that lived on the farm from wandering too far and getting themselves mixed up with the animals from other farms. Secondly, they stopped wild animals like leopards, lions and wild dogs from coming into the farm. The fences needed frequent inspection and maintenance and the quickest and easiest way of doing this, was on horseback. So, as soon as Nelson was big enough, when he was about 2 years old, he had to be taught how to carry a human on his back and that is when the problem arose.

The trouble with Nelson was that he had always been a very stubborn horse. Bella said that he got this stubborn streak from his father, but I am not so sure about that. I have known her to be equally headstrong when it came to it.

The task of schooling Nelson was left to little Louis, who was once again on holiday from school. He just had his 16th birthday and was not so little anymore. He was nearly as tall as Mr Le Roux. It was decided by Ezra and Mr Le Roux, that he was now strong enough to do the job.

'He knows the horse well and they trust each other. I don't think he'll have too much trouble,' said Mr Le Roux.

Louis came into the Paddock with a bridle and placed it over Nelson's head. Once secure, he was led out into the farmyard, where Louis placed the saddle on his back and fastened it under his belly. As soon as this was done, Nelson turned his back on Louis and started back to the paddock. Louis pulled him back by the reins.

'And, where do you think you are going?' asked Louis. 'Wooa! Stand still!'

Nelson looked at me: 'I don't think I am going to like this very much.'

'Don't be so silly, Nelson, you're a big, strong horse, quite capable of carrying anybody on your back.'

'All the same,' said Nelson. 'I think I will play a few tricks on him.'

Mr Le Roux and Ezra were looking on from a distance.

'The honey needs taking out of the beehives this afternoon,' said Ezra.

'So?' asked Mr Le Roux.

'I don't like doing it,' said Ezra. 'Those little devils have sharp tails.'

'Mm,' said Mr Le Roux. 'I know what you mean.'

'So, you don't think Master Louis will have any problems?' asked Ezra.

'No. I shouldn't think so,' replied Mr Le Roux. 'Remember I taught him to ride myself.'

'Mm,' said Ezra. 'I say Master Louis will fly like an eagle today. If I'm right, you see to the bees. If you're right, I'll fight with them.'

'Mm,' said Mr Le Roux. 'You're on.'

Louis placed his left foot in the stirrup and heaved himself into the saddle. It was just as the seat of his pants touched the saddle that all hell broke loose. Nelson bent his knees and shot straight up into the air. On the way down he ducked his head between his front legs. As soon as his feet hit the ground, he kicked high with his hind legs. Louis, who was still surprised in mid-air, got the full impact of the rising saddle on his backside. There was a blur of khaki shorts and white shirt as he did a somersault and then he hit the ground with a dull thud.

'Mm,' said Ezra.

'Mm,' said Mr Le Roux.

'Uh!' grunted Louis.

Nelson looked at me and grinned: 'How did you like that then, Dilly?'

'I think you are being very silly,' said I. 'You could have hurt the boy. What has he ever done to you?'

Louis got up off the ground and dusted himself down. His injured pride would not allow him to back off. He was determined to have another go, but this time he did not even stand a chance of reaching the saddle. He placed his foot in the stirrup, but as soon as his other foot left the ground, Nelson jumped to the right and then to the left, slamming into Louis's midriff. Once again the boy went sprawling; Winded and bruised.

'Mm,' said Ezra.

He walked over to Louis and helped him to his feet.

'What is the matter with him, Ezra?' asked Louis.

'All Satan's children are in him,' said Ezra. 'Let's bring out the mule and see if he can talk some sense into him.'

He opened the gate and led me out into the yard to stand next to Nelson.

'Now! Will you behave yourself?' said I.

'Oh, all right, then,' said Nelson. 'But, I am telling you now. I am not doing any of this carrying lark unless you come with me.'

'Now, try him again,' said Ezra. 'He will be fine. The mule has had a word with him.'

'Don't be silly, Ezra,' said Louis. 'I don't trust him. Maybe you should have a go.'

'No Master Louis. I'm telling you. He will behave now.'

Gingerly, Louis approached Nelson and stroked his neck. Nelson nuzzled him with his nose. Once again Louis placed his foot in the stirrup and raised himself into the saddle. Calmly, Nelson began to walk and then trot, with me by his side.

Oh! What Freedom!

Although I scolded Nelson severely for his behaviour, I was secretly rather pleased. Because from that day, I had the run of the farm.

'Mm,' said Mr Le Roux.

'Now, Sir,' said Ezra. 'I will go and prune the trees, while you see to the bees.'

At first I would only gallop by Nelson's side while he was being ridden, but soon Ezra had another one of his good ideas.

'What is the point in allowing that idle mule just to run about like this? He might as well earn his keep.'

So, he put a saddle on me and rode on my back. From then on, whenever two people were required to do a job away from home, Nelson and I would be used to carry the humans. Oh! What fun! I ran for all I was worth! I looked and I learned!

And, in this manner, the first two years of my life drew to a close.

III. RAISINS

Christmas time was approaching and everything was hustle and bustle on the farm. All the humans were very excited and their agitation was transmitted to the animals. Nelson, Bella and I had a light spring in our step. We craned our necks over the paddock fence and listened to the chatter in the farm yard.

Mr And Mrs Le Roux were discussing the arrangements for the big day and Louis and Bess were talking about the new clothes they would need for the occasion. Rachael was talking about all the cooking that needed to be done and Ezra? Well, Ezra. He went about his duties – cool, calm and collected and undisturbed by it all. Let me tell you a little about our friend Ezra.

Nothing much seemed to bother Ezra. When all around him turned to chaos, he would stand in the middle of it all, sometimes smiling, sometimes thoughtful, but always as reliable as a baobab tree. While others rushed about, he would observe life from a distance and when he had discovered the flaws, he would move in with a graceful step and smooth all the rough edges and restore sanity. And, most of all, he understood animals better than any other human. He was our friend.

Every year, on Christmas day, all the neighbouring farmers and their families would get together on one of the farms. This year it was our turn to organise the celebrations. Bella, Nelson and I were always treated with special consideration by the humans. We were more like friends of the family than working animals. Maybe this was due to the difficult circumstances of my birth. Be that as it may, the paddock gate was frequently left open and we were allowed to wander in the farm-yard. Of course we knew this was a perfect opportunity to join in all the fun.

The day before Christmas though, something rather peculiar happened whilst we were strolling around the yard. The chicken coop was left open and all the hens and the big rooster, Sam, were grubbing in the dust. Rachael came out of the kitchen with a large enamel bucket and left it outside the back-door. After she had gone back inside, we casually walked over to have a look at the contents of the bucket. It seemed to be filled with millions of shrivelled little fruit. I stuck my nose in it and had a sniff.

'Oh, Nelson! Bella! Come and smell this! This smells better than a green pasture! Better than the most succulent grass! Better than a barn full of fresh hay!'

'It does indeed smell nice,' said Bella. 'I wonder if we should just have a little taste.'

I stuck out my tongue and lapped up a few of the fruit. It was succulently sweet. Fumes rose from the bucket up my nose, making my head spin. Soon we were all tucking in. We just could not stop ourselves. In fact, we went at it so hard that we knocked the bucket over.

'Oomph,' said Sam the rooster, strolling up and clearing his throat. 'That does look rather appetizing. Will you two gents and the good lady allow me and my wives to partake of your feast?'

Sam always spoke in this manner. He fancied himself as a lady's man.

'Most certainly,' said Bella. 'Just help yourselves.'

Oh, what a feast! What a feast! I can honestly say that I have never tasted anything like that since.

'I wonder,' said I, my cheeks bulging, 'what this fruit ish? Maybe there ish shome more in the kitchen. Maybe we should go and have a look.'

'We are not allowed to go into the housh,' said Bella.

'Oh, never mind zat,' said I. 'I am an old dear friend of the family. There is absholutely nothing that I cannot do. Hick! Hick!'

'Wery eloquently put, young shir,' said Sam. 'I think that ish a most exchellent idea. I persheve you to be a young man of courage and valour, jusht like meshelf.'

I looked at Bella and Nelson and I was mildly surprised to see that there were two Bella's and two Nelsons.

'There are four of you. Hick!' said I.

'There are two of you. Hick!' said Bella.

'Well, never mind, then,' said I. 'Let ush all go and shee whatsh happening in the kitchen.'

We strolled over to the kitchen. Well. I say stroll, but it was more of a stumble than a stroll. You see, there were so many of us that we got in each other's way.

I stuck my head round the door.

'There ish nobody here. Follow me. Let'sh enter and shee wat'sh cooking.'

'Ah! Mosht droll! Mosht droll!' said Sam from behind us in the yard. 'With humoush remarksh like that you will achieve lofty hightsh, rather like meshelf. Hick!'

We pushed our way into the kitchen and I looked at all the old familiar sights. There was the old stove, the large oak kitchen table and chairs, the tall dresser and large armchair, all in exactly the same places as they were when I had lived there.

'What ish that?' asked the two Nelsons, looking at the stove.

'That ish a shtove,' said I. 'The humansh put water and food on it before they eat it.'

'Why?' asked the two Nelsons.

'I am really totally unable to give a coherent ansher to your queshtion,' said I.

'My!' said the two Bella's. 'But, you have the mosht beautiful command of the shpoken word.'

The six of us staggered over to the stove.

'I think I will take a sheat for a moment,' said the two Nelsons.

'What a shplendid idea,' said I. 'I think I will join you.'

Soon the six of us were crouching on our hind legs in front of the stove. A little door in the stove was standing half open. From behind this a red glow could be seen.

'What'sh that?' asked the two Nelsons.

'That'sh called fire,' said I.

'What ish fire?' asked the two Nelsons.

'I don't really know,' said I.

'I think I will have a shniff at it,' said the two Nelsons and they promptly stuck their noses in through the little door and that is when everything started to go drastically wrong.

There was an appalling smell and then a redness appeared around their heads. Then, there was an awful lot of smoke and the locks of hair on their foreheads disappeared. The two Nelsons jumped up and something large and unspeakable appeared behind them on the floor.

Then, there were Nelsons everywhere! Chairs were crashing about; cups and saucers were raining from the sky and all the Nelsons were shouting like a herd possessed.

That was when Mrs Le Roux and Rachael appeared on the scene. Oh, my life! What a noise there was! Animal shouts, mingled with human screams! We were all running about now in the confined space of the kitchen. We were bumping and pushing each other and the sound of our hoof-beats shook the walls.

'Ezra! Danie! Quick! Help! Oh my god! Help!' shouted Mrs Le Roux.

A minute later Ezra and Mr Le Roux appeared from the direction of the dining-room. Nelson was running round and round the kitchen in circles and Bella and I followed him closely. Mr Le Roux jumped in front of Nelson and tried to stop him, but he was unceremoniously barged out of the way.

Then, Ezra decided to take command. I could not swear to it, but I think I saw a little glint in his eye and a flicker of a smile around his mouth. Anyway, he quickly pulled Rachael and Mr and Mrs Le Roux out of the way and pushed them into the dining-room and banged the door shut.

Then, he went and stood in the middle of the kitchen, facing the back-door, while we ran around him. For a while he just stood there and watched us. He was waiting for the right moment. Then, suddenly, as Nelson came round once more and just as he was level with Ezra and the back-door, he shot out a large fist which connected with a dull thud on the side of Nelson's jaw. Nelson's head jerked to the left and he saw the open door in front of him and he shot through it into the open yard, with Bella and I close on his heels.

Behind us the human chaos continued. Mr Le Roux emerged from the kitchen door, followed by the two women and Ezra. It is funny how many colours human beings can display when they get cross. Mr Le Roux was as red as a beetroot and he was shaking his fist and shouting at us. Rachael was grey like ash. She was clinging to the door-frame and her knees were shaking. Mrs Le Roux was as white as a sheet, but it was not from shock. She was just so very angry with us.

'Look!' she shrieked. She pointed at the yard. 'Just look at what they have done to my chickens! They have killed them all! That is it! These animals will have to go! Get rid of them! I don't care where they go! Just get rid of them!'

Only Ezra appeared to be calm. As we disappeared into the distance, jumping the steel-wire fences, he was staring after us with a strange, dream-like expression on his face.

If those who knew him well had bothered to observe him, they would have noticed a gleam of humour in his eyes which gradually turned to contemplative speculation. It was obvious that a wonderful thought had entered his sharp mind.

'Ezra! Stir yourself! Do something about my chickens!' Mrs Le Roux was crouching in the dust next to Sam.

Ezra shook himself as if he was returning from a deep dream and walked over to the bucket.

'They will be alright,' he said calmly. 'They have just helped themselves to the raisins from the ginger beer.'

He picked up Sam and tossed him into the air. Sam gave a sort of hoarse, stuttering crow, landed on a branch of the mulberry tree and tumbled backwards and landed in a flurry of feathers and a puff of dust on his back.

"Wow!' said Ezra. He will have one very bad headache.

Gradually, the chaos subsided. The chickens were gathered up and stacked in the coop and Mrs Le Roux and Rachael retired to the kitchen where they got down to cleaning and scrubbing.

Although still greatly annoyed, Mr Le Roux returned to a normal colour. He was leaning on the fence, looking in the direction in which we had disappeared. Ezra came and stood next to him.

'The races are in May,' he said in measured tones.

'What are you on about, Ezra?' Mr Le Roux looked at him as if he had gone crazy. 'What on earth are you on about?'

'Nelson jumped that fence well. He flew like a bird. And, did you see the mule? We will get a good price on him. There are no rules about raisins.'

Mr Le Roux looked at him in wonder:

'Ezra! I hope you are not suggesting...! I hope I did not understand you correctly! I hope ...' His voice trailed off. 'When is the race meeting?'

'The first week in May.'

'Mm,' said Mr Le Roux.

'Mm,' said Ezra.

'We must keep very quiet about what happened here today. You talk to Rachael and I will have a word with Mrs Le Roux. If we should win the races, we do not want people suddenly to start talking and accusing us of cheating, do we?'

'I agree,' said Ezra. 'That would not be very good.'

Later that day, Ezra and Mr Le Roux had a word with the women. As Ezra put it:

'We do not want those good-for-nothing layabouts, who work for Mr de Vries to snigger behind their hands at us. We do not want to become the laughing-stock of the neighbourhood. So, I think it is better that we keep a quiet tongue in our mouths.'

Grudgingly, the women agreed and later that evening, we came skulking back to the paddock. Ezra brought us a large bunch of carrots, which did not please Rachael.

'Those animals destroyed my kitchen and you feed them? The little brains you have must have gone soft.

'We do not want them to become ill, do we?' said Ezra. 'This will soak up some of the beer in their bellies.'

While Ezra fed us the carrots, he spoke quietly to us and we could tell that he was rather pleased about something.

The next day was Christmas day and people arrived from all the neighbouring farms, dressed in their finest clothes. They arrived by all forms of transport: Carts, wagons, trucks and some even came on horseback.

All the horses were put in the paddock with Bella, Nelson and me. There was one particularly large, white horse which stood tall on slender legs. His name was Samson and all the other horses seemed to be in awe of him. He was telling stories about all the races that he had won and how he was going to win the next race. Nelson and I didn't like him very much.

'He is a very boastful horse,' said Nelson. 'I wish I could run fast. I would like to stick all his stories back down his throat.'

Ah! If Nelson only knew! His chance to do this would happen sooner than he thought.

The farm-yard and the house were crowded with humans. The older people were sitting on the veranda, drinking tea and the younger humans gathered in the yard under the mulberry trees, drinking beer and chattering.

At midday everybody gathered in the big, front room and all went silent. One man stood up and talked to the others and told them a story about a child that was born a long time ago. This was a very special child that was called Jesus, and he would save everybody, from what, I could not quite understand, but it sounded like a nice story.

We could see them all sitting in the house and since the windows were left open, we could hear everything that was said. Then they all sang a song and the meeting broke up.

By this time Rachael and Mrs Le Roux had finished cooking and everybody prepared themselves for the midday feast. There were so many people that not everyone could eat around the big table in the dining-room. So, the young people all sat on rugs on the lawn in front of the house.

And so, the day progressed until it was time for all to go home. One by one, the trucks, the carts and the wagons left the yard. The horses were saddled and ridden away and soon the paddock and the yard were completely empty. Christmas day had ended.

We watched Ezra and Mr Le Roux walking off in the direction of the big dam and the cattle trough. The cows had to be watered and milked. The farm had become quiet again and I thought to myself that this was how I liked it best. It was quite exciting having all those people and animals around for a day, but there was nothing in the world as restful and calm as an African farm at dusk.

IV. RACE

I came awake slowly from a deep sleep and a dream. I was not sure what I dreamt about, but I knew that I had this dream before. I knew that my mother was with me and she was trying to tell me something. Something that happened a very long time ago. I was to have the dream again, but the subject of the dream is another story that I will tell later.

It was still night, but I knew that dawn was just around the corner of the darkness. What had awakened me? I stood and listened. It was very quiet. All the little night creatures were going into hiding from the coming light and none of the day creatures were stirring yet. A few stars were still clinging to the night, but they would soon retreat before the rising sun.

Then I heard it again: A long, drawn-out shriek as of some creature in agony. It was that confounded Sam! I would have to talk to Ezra and ask him if it was at all possible to make some kind of a muzzle for the foul cockerel to stop him from crowing so early in the morning. I saw him one morning when he bellowed like that and the horrid brute was still asleep while he crowed. I knew from previous experience that he would carry on like this for a few minutes and that he would then keep quiet for another half hour or so. Then, he would howl again for a few minutes and once again he would go back to sleep. After another period, he would crow again, but by this time, he would have woken every animal and humans for miles around. Confounded creature!

Nelson Stamped his foot: 'What that chicken deserves, is a good kicking! Don't be too surprised if a little accident should happen one of these days.'

'You just leave old Sam alone,' said Bella. 'He is a real gentleman and you should respect his age.'

'Gentleman, my hoof!' grunted Nelson. 'He's just a dirty old cockerel! He never does anything useful around the place! Just listen to that racket!'

After a little while, Sam went back to sleep and the three of us plucked idly at the dewy grass at our feet.

'Incidentally. Do you know what day it is today?' asked Bella.

'Saturday,' grumbled Nelson.

'No. I don't mean what day of the week. Do you know what is happening today? It is the day we leave for the races and you better get yourself into a better mood and pull yourself together. You are racing in the big one tomorrow.'

'Oh, yes,' said Nelson. I completely forgot. That braggart, Samson, will be there. I would like to kick some dust in his face.'

'You will have your work cut out against him, my lad. He is an Arabian stallion.'

'We'll see,' said Nelson. Where is Arabia? Never heard of it. Anyway. So what! I am a stallion from Botswana. So there. Let us try and get a little more sleep. I am going to need my beauty sleep and all my strength.'

'Humph!' Bella blew disdainfully through her nose. 'Beauty sleep indeed! We all noticed how interested you were in that little mare of Mr Andersons at Christmas; you couldn't keep your eyes off her. You are becoming as bad as old Sam!'

Nelson just snorted in disgust and turned his back on Bella. We dozed off for another hour or so, until Sam started shrieking again.

And we resigned ourselves to the fact that we were not going to get any more rest.

I looked up and saw that the stars were leaving us, making room for the sun, which was just poking its red face over the edge of the world. I heard the kitchen door opening and Mr Le Roux appeared, dressed in an old khaki shirt and trousers and a pair of scruffy old boots. In his mouth, he had his pipe and on his head, was that floppy old hat. Mr Le Roux never went anywhere without his hat, or his pipe. They were sort of part of him. Sometimes he did not even realise that he had these articles on his person. Let me give you an example.

One day, we were out repairing fences. When the work was done, all the tools were collected and loaded onto the back of the truck. Then, Mr Le Roux started walking up and down in a very agitated way. He appeared to be looking for something in the long grass.

'What are you looking for, Dad?' asked Louis.

'My pipe,' said Mr Le Roux. 'I must have dropped it somewhere.'

'Are you sure it is not on your person?' asked Louis, smiling broadly.

'I am positive.' He took his pipe out of his mouth and pointed. 'I thought I had left it on that stone over there when we put the last post in.'

Anyway, just now he was wandering off in the direction of the kraal *19. Since the paddock gate was left open, Bella, Nelson and I ambled into the yard and followed him down the path.

The milk cows were just beginning to stir. Soon, Ezra and the other farm workers also arrived. They each carried a bucket and a leather thong. It was time for milking.

Milking the cows is one of those activities which has to take place every single day of the year. If the cows are not milked regularly, they become very uncomfortable. When I was young, the cows still had to be milked by hand. These days, they use machines with tubes and suckers which are attached to the teats to do the milking. Each person positioned himself next to a cow and placed a bucket between the hind legs of the cow. Then, holding a teat in each hand, the milkers would squeeze and pull, squirting hot, foaming milk into a bucket. A lovely, warm, sweet smell would fill the air. The milkers had to be careful not to milk all the teats. One had to be left for the calf.

While the cows were being milked, young Louis arrived. He was responsible for separating the cream from the milk. There was a little brick-built room where this was done.

Inside this little room, stood a stone pillar with a funny looking machine bolted to the top. On one side of the machine, was a handle that could be turned.

Louis began to assemble the separators which were fitted to the top of the machine. The separators consisted of loads of tiny metal bowls with a hole in the bottom of each and 3 holes in the side of each. These bowls were fitted, one inside the other and placed upside down on a spindle on top of the machine. When the handle was turned, the bowls would spin very rapidly. Milk would be poured into the little spinning bowls and forced out through the holes in the side, thus causing the cream to separate from the milk.

After the separating had been done, the cream was poured into metal churns and stored in a cooler. Every Tuesday a man would come to the farm and load the cream onto a big truck and take it away to the dairy, which was in a town about 300 miles away from the farm.

After milking and separating, all the equipment were thoroughly washed and stored away and Louis and Mr Le Roux went back to the house for breakfast. Although it was only 8 o'clock, work on the farm had been in progress for three hours or more.

After breakfast, the day to day work on the farm carried on as normal. Ezra went off to the north dam to water the garden, Little Louis went to help mend a fence and Mr Le Roux was mending the drive-belt on the pump engine at the south dam.

Let me tell you a bit about the work on the farm in those early days.

In the north garden, Mrs Le Roux grew some fruits and vegetables. These included apricots, guavas, lemons, figs, tomatoes, lettuce, cabbage, carrots and, best of all, prickly pears. We animals were constantly in trouble for wandering into the garden and chomping our way through the cabbages and the prickly pears. Every day, before the sun got too hot, somebody had to go and water the fruit trees and the vegetable patches.

In those days, there was no piped water on the farm. A series of ditches were dug, leading from the dam and ending in the different vegetable beds and underneath the fruit trees. A large tap on the side of the dam was turned on and water flowed along the irrigation ditches to the vegetables and fruit. This was Ezra's job on this particular morning.

Louis went off with some farmworkers to mend a fence. As I have already told you, the fences served two purposes: Firstly, they kept the animals from wandering all over the farm and also to stop them from straying into the bush-veldt. The second purpose of the fences was to keep wild animals, such as wild dogs, lions and jackals from coming onto the farm and attacking the farm animals.

Most often, repairing the fence involved replacing the rotten fence post. To replace a post, a straight, young tree had to be found and chopped down. All the branches were trimmed away, but the bark was left on the post, because it acted as extra protection from the weather. The old post was then dug out and the new post was bedded into position and the strands of fence wire were attached to the new post.

Both the north dam and the south dam on the farm were filled with water from wells. Over each well stood a windmill which pumped the water from the wells into the dams. When there was no wind, water was pumped from the wells with a pump engine. A long, circular belt ran from a wheel on the pump engine to a wheel on the windmill and quite often this belt broke and had to be repaired. This was Mr Le Roux's job on this particular morning.

While the men were away at their work, Bella, Nelson and I stood idly in our paddock and watched the activity in the farm-yard. Rachael came out of the kitchen with a bag of maize. She opened the chicken coop and scattered some maize on the ground in the yard. All the chickens came out and started grubbing in the sand for food. Rachael went into the coop and appeared a few minutes later, the bag now filled with fresh eggs.

Old Sam jumped up onto the window-sill of the kitchen and sat there, staring at something inside the house. After a while, he jumped down and strolled over to the paddock.

'Good morning, good lady and gentlemen. And, how are you all on this auspicious day?'

'Morning, Sam,' said Nelson. 'And, what exactly does "auspicious" mean?'

'Uh-uh!' Sam cleared his throat. 'Glad you asked, Lad. Always happy to instruct a young buck like you in the higher formalities of life. "Auspicious" means: "of good omen or promising."'

'Oh, really,' said Nelson. 'And, by the way. I am not a buck. I am a horse. A buck means: ""The male of various kind of deer, rabbit, hare, etc."'

'Shut up, Nelson,' said Bella. 'Don't mind him, Sam. Forgive his rudeness and tell us what you saw in the kitchen.'

'Oh, my dear lady! I saw something totally delectable in the kitchen.'

'What does "delect--"'

'Shut up, Nelson. What did you see in the kitchen?'

'Well. Remember when we ate that funny fruit and I had the most beautiful sleep during the day and I woke up and I thought the earth had dropped on my head? Well! There is another bucket full of that fruit on the kitchen table. Now, what do you think of that?'

'Not a lot,' said Nelson. 'If I remember correctly, the animal population of this yard doubled for some mysterious reason, within a matter of minutes. There were horses, mules and fowl everywhere! I didn't mind the horses and the mules too much, but I have enough trouble with the confounded fowl under my feet. I definitely don't want them to double in numbers.'

'I have told you already, Nelson! Don't be so rude to Sam! You are not too old to get a good kicking!' Bella stamped her foot in annoyance.

'Never mind, dear lady. As somebody once said: "Youth is wasted on the young". I know that he really admires me and his remarks are just spurious utterances.'

'Oomph,' grunted Nelson.

I couldn't resist it: 'What does "spuri--".

'Shut up, Dilly!' shouted Bella. 'Well, thank you for giving us your news, Sam. It is greatly appreciated. You keep a sharp eye out and let us know what is happening.'

'More like a beady eye,' grunted Nelson under his breath and Sam strolled back to his wives.

Well, suffice it to say, in view of what happened before, Mrs Le Roux was not so foolish as to leave the bucket of fruit outside the house again.

Just after midday the men appeared from their respective work and they all had lunch. After lunch, Mr Le Roux walked round the corner of the house and sat himself down with a book in the shade of a tree. He did this every afternoon when the sun was at its hottest and he would read for an hour or so. Well, he told everybody that he was going to read, but from what I knew of humans, he read in the most peculiar way. He would open the book, glance at it for a minute, close his eyes, put his head against the back-rest of the chair and start to breathe in a rumbling sort of way. Most strange.

After an hour or so, Mr Le Roux stood up and came back into the yard.

'Had a good read?' asked Mrs Le Roux.

'Ah! Very good! Most interesting.'

'Oh, really,' said Mrs Le Roux. 'You must tell me what the book is about sometime. If I am not mistaken, you have been reading that book for the last two years.'

'Well, never mind that,' said Mr Le Roux. 'We have got to get ready for the races. Where is my pipe and my hat?"

'Your pipe is in your left hand and your hat is on your head,' said Mrs Le Roux.

'Ah! So it is! I think Louis and Ezra can take the horses over to Mr Steyn's place tonight. We can leave early tomorrow morning.'

'Are you entering the mule as well?' asked Mrs Le Roux.

'Yes. Why not? Anyway, you know Nelson won't go anywhere without him. You never know. The mule may surprise us.'

During the afternoon, Louis and Ezra brought the saddles and reins into the yard. They also brought a large number of flat bits of brass with beautiful patterns on them. They spent the afternoon polishing the saddles and the brasses until they shone brightly in the afternoon sun.

'Come here, you two,' said Ezra to Nelson and me. 'Let's smarten you up a bit.'

We were brushed and groomed until we shone nearly as brightly as the brasses and then we were dressed up in our shiny new clothes.

"Oh, goodness me! The two of you look absolutely stunning!' said Bella.

'Most handsome,' said Sam. 'I must admit that you look nearly as pucker as meself.'

'Two other horses were coming with us. There was a young mare called Sadie and a young stallion named Stroller.

At about 4 o'clock we set off for Mr Steyn's farm. Ezra was on Nelson's back, Louis was riding me and the two other horses came behind, led on reins.

'Good luck, you two,' said Bella. 'And, Nelson! Just behave yourself!'

'Good luck,' said Sam. 'May you bring honour and distinction to this illustrious farm.'

So, off we went.

We Reached Mr Steyn's farm at about 7 o'clock in the evening. Many humans and horses were already assembled on the camp-site that was set up for the night. Horses were being groomed and fed and camp-fires were lit and food was prepared for the humans. There was a general hustle and bustle and everybody was very excited. The humans were inspecting each other's horses and all the talk was about the next day's races.

At about 11 o'clock, blankets were spread on the ground and all the humans went to sleep.

Early the next morning, Mr Le Roux, Mrs Le Roux, young Bess and Rachael arrived. The fires that had burnt down during the night were rekindled and the humans fed on porridge and strong coffee.

The morning was spent on preparation. Saddles and brasses were once again polished, horses were once again groomed and the fences for the races were erected. In the old farmhouse, food and drink were prepared and carried out and placed on large trestle tables by the side of the race-course.

At another large table, a man settled himself with books and pieces of paper and a metal box full of money. He was taking bets on the different horses. By 11 o'clock all was ready and the first race was under way. There was little interest from the Le Roux contingent in the first two races. However, Stroller came a creditable second in the third race and then Sadie, who was running in the young mares, won her race. She was so pleased with herself, after the race, she pranced about like a young foal. The fifth race came and went, but we were so excited that we didn't even notice, because Nelson and I were running in the sixth and last race of the day. It was a two-miler, the longest event of the day.

A strange thing happened while the fifth race was in progress. While everybody's attention was on the running horses, Ezra came over to Nelson with a nose-bag and tied it around his neck. 'Strange,' I thought to myself. 'As far as I am aware, horses don't normally get fed just before a race.'

'What's in the bag, Nelson?' I asked.

'You'd never believe it, Dilly! It is some of that beautiful fruit that we had a few weeks ago.'

With-in a matter of seconds, he had gobbled up all the fruit and Ezra had removed the bag. Nobody had noticed.

A few minutes later, we were led to the starting line. Ezra was to ride on Nelson and Louis on me.

'How do you feel, Nelson?' I asked.

'Absholutely fantastic!' said Nelson.

'Why are you speaking in that funny way?' I asked him.

'I am not shpeaking in a funny way, hick!' answered Nelson. 'I am exsheedingly eloquent.'

I was worried. Nelson was sounding a little bit like Sam.

The starter lowered his flag and the race was off. Because it was such a long race, we kept a steady pace for the first three-quarters of a mile. Samson was lying second, with Nelson and I just behind. It was at the fifteenth fence, about a mile from home that the trouble occurred. I had an inkling that something was wrong when Nelson said to me that he could see two Samson's in front of him.

'Which one am I shupposed to raish againsht? He asked me.

'Don't be so silly,' said I. 'There is only one Samson.'

'No. Really. There are two of them,' He replied.

'Well,' said I, 'In that case I would just run between the two of them.'

I should never have told him to do that! To this day I still hold myself responsible for the disastrous events which followed.

The pace had picked up and Samson was now out in front with Nelson just behind him. I had fallen right back, but I could see the two of them out in front. The fifteenth fence was coming up fast. Samson lifted his tail and jumped and at the same time Nelson launched himself like an arrow out of a bow. Samson jumped far and high, but Nelson jumped further and higher and unfortunately, he took my advice. He tried to jump between the two mythical Samson's. As they reached the top of the arc above the fence, Nelson drilled his nose deep in between Samson's ample buttocks with an almighty force. Samson hit the ground with quivering legs. Nelson's momentum carried the two of them along for another few yards before they both collapsed, flailing in the dust.

The rest of the riders and horses, who were all bunched behind the two fallers, looked on, first, in stunned silence and then with hoops of laughter. Not one horse took the fence cleanly. Most of them fell and those who did not just gave up. The riders were laughing so much that they could not continue with the race. That is, except for Louis and I. We were so far back in the field, Louis had time to take stock of the situation. We jumped the fence and the subsequent fences and cantered home. We reached the finishing line and I have never heard so much cheering and laughter as on that day.

There was obviously an inquest into the events afterwards, but no firm conclusion was reached. Anyway, everybody enjoyed what had happened so much that nobody could take it very seriously.

Later that afternoon, before returning home, I overheard a conversation between Ezra and Mr Le Roux.

'Well, Ezra. That was not very clever,' said Mr Le Roux. 'We lost an awful lot of money. I put £100 on Nelson at 3 to 1.'

'Mm,' said Ezra.

'Mm,' said Mr Le Roux.

'Nobody gave the mule a chance,' said Ezra. 'I felt sorry for him. I put £10 on him at 150 to 1.'

Ezra strolled away and Mr Le Roux's jaw dropped and his pipe fell out of his mouth.

Since that day, Samson never took part in another race. I did hear a rumour that he became very nervous in the company of other horses, especially stallions. Especially when approached   from   behind.

V. EXIT

It is evening. It is that time, just before the sun is setting. Nelson and I are quietly grazing in the paddock. In the distance we can hear the voices of the farm workers. They have finished their day's labour and are chatting happily as they make their way home. It has been a long, hot day and they are looking forward to their rest after the day's labour and their evening meal.

After some time, we see Louis Le Roux and Ezra approaching the house. They are both carrying buckets of milk and they are quietly chatting about the passing day and the things that needed to be done tomorrow. Mr. Le Roux retired some time ago and he and his wife decided to go travelling. Louis is a young man now and he is running the farm.

Nelson and I are alone. We have been on our own for a few years now. Bella died some years ago. She was quite old, but I believe she had a happy life. She was well looked after by everybody on the farm and all her life she looked after Nelson and me and she shared in our many adventures.

Nelson and I are of a similar age and we do understand each other very well. We don't have to talk to one another anymore. We just put our heads together and our thoughts just pass between us. Like we are having a thought conversation.

Nelson says: 'You know, Dilly. I really am beginning to feel quite old and tired. I can't run about as much as I used to.'

'I agree,' says I. 'I would really like to have a long rest. But, I am afraid that I would not see you, or the farm, or all the humans and other animals again if I should have this long rest.'

'I know what you mean,' says Nelson. 'But, you know. I have a notion that we will meet again in a different life. Remember those stories that the humans always tell each other? Tales about something called heaven and angels, someone called God, and an afterlife? Do you think they're right? They are all very clever, you know. They must know what they are talking about. Maybe we will meet in this "afterlife".'

'Oh, yes, Nelson. I think you may be right! Anyway, we have had a very good life here on the farm. I have so many good memories from the days when we were young. Do you remember when Louis first got on your back and you threw him off? And, do you remember when we went into the kitchen after we ate all that fruit?'

'Oh, yes,' says Nelson. 'I do remember. And, I also remember the headache I had afterwards.'

'Oh, Nelson! Do you remember the race when you stuck your nose up ...'

'Dilly!' says Nelson. 'I would rather not talk about that. That is one of my worst memories.'

We carry on grazing and talking for some time. Eventually the sun goes down and the moon shows its smiling face in the sky. We fall silent and after some time we lie down on the grass and go to sleep.

****

I am in a foreign land. I do not know how I know it, but I am certain that it is a very long time ago. I am tethered to a post next to a small dwelling. I know that my master lives inside.

In the distance I can see a high wall with an archway and a gate. I know there are many people living and working behind that wall. It is called a "city".

The road to the city gate passes my master's dwelling. There is a constant flow of traffic to and from the city along this road. Most of the people are walking, but some of them are riding on the backs of donkeys. Some of the people are leading their donkeys. These animals are heavily laden with baskets of fruit, or meat, or bread.

My master comes out of the dwelling. He is carrying some wooden stakes. These he bangs into the earth with a large mallet. He goes back inside and returns with some wooden boards which he lies upon the stakes, thus creating a long table. He then proceeds to lay some wares on the table: Jars of wine, loaves of bread, a variety of cheeses, baskets of fruit and chunks of meat. He positions himself next to the table and, ringing a hand-bell, he attracts the attention of the passing people. The rest of the day he spends on haggling and bartering with the passersby, but being a consummate salesman, he is sure to make a decent profit.

Sometime during the afternoon, we become aware of a disturbance in the distance. There is the noise of a crowd of people singing, shouting and cheering. Then, as we watch, a group of people materialise along the road. As they come closer, we notice that their attention is focused on a young man in their centre.

As they reach our position, the young man holds up his hand and his companions come to a halt. He leaves the crowd and makes his way to my master's stand. My master appears to recognise the man. He smiles broadly and bows. They have a short conversation, but since it is so noisy, I can't hear what they are saying to each other.

After a little, my master walks towards me and unties the rope from the post. He leads me to the young man who places a gentle hand upon my back.

I don't know quite how to describe what happens next. As he touches me, a feeling of peace and serenity passes through me. I trust him with all my being. Then, with the help of my master, he climbs lightly onto my back. I am surprised at how light he appears to be. But, then, I realise that my whole body is filled with boundless energy.

My master leads me back to the road and we join the young man's companions. Then, we turn towards the city gates. We pass through the arch, enter the city and make our way to a large square where the young man dismounts. He thanks my master and we make our way back to his stall where he continues to sell his wares.

In the late afternoon, a man approaches the stall. I recognise him as one of those who had been in the group with the young man who had entered the city on my back; He points at some jars of wine and a few loaves of bread and he gives my master some coins. Then he gives some directions and he asks if the wares could be delivered later that evening.

So, at the end of the day, my master dismantles his stall and stores his goods in his dwelling. Then he fills some baskets with bread and jars of wine. These he place on my back and we make our way along a narrow road to a distant hill. Along the way we pass through some olive groves. I have never seen olives before, but I just know what they are. At last we reach the top of the hill and we find ourselves by a big house. My master knocks on the door which is opened by a man. My master unties the baskets of wine and bread from my back and they carry these into the house. I look through a window and see a group of men sitting around a table. At the head of the table sits the young man who had been riding on my back earlier in the day. The bread and wine is placed on the table and my master leaves the house and returns to where I am standing.

We leave our position at the window, but my master seems reluctant to depart. So, we move some distance from the house, where we stop. We turn round and we find that we can still see the crowd sitting around the table by the candlelight.

The young man takes the bread, breaks it and passes it to the others. He speaks to them and they eat in silence. Then, he pours wine into little bowls and once again he passes these to his friends. After a few words from him, they drink the wine.

It is then that something rather disturbing happens. He appears to have words with one specific man. This individual seems upset by what is said to him. He jumps up and leaves the house and rushes into the darkness down the path that leads to the city.

My master and I remain where we are. It is as if he is waiting for something else to happen and he is right. In less than an hour, we hear a commotion and we see some lights approaching along the path. A group of men appear and they make their way towards the house. They look like soldiers.

The group inside become aware of those outside and they leave the table and come out of the house to see what it is all about. The man who left in a temper earlier goes up to the young man and kisses him on both cheeks. This is obviously a sign to the soldiers. They move forward, grab the young man and proceed to bind his hands. One of the followers of the young man draws his sword and challenges the soldiers, but his master speaks to him and he puts his sword away. The soldiers make their way back from where they had appeared and we all follow them down the road at a distance.

When we get back to the city, my master decides that we should go home. Maybe he thinks that he had seen enough. He seems thoughtful and somewhat depressed. When we get home, he tethers me outside and he goes into his dwelling, to sleep.

It is morning. My master appears. As is the usual, he installs his tables and arranges his wares upon it. He rings his bell intermittently and he calls to the passersby to come and sample the wine and food. Soon he is busy and all is back to a normal day's activities.

Business carries on until early noon. Then, we become aware of a disturbance behind the city walls. It is the sound of people shouting. At first it seems to be a long distance off, but gradually the noise increases and we gather from this that the crowd is moving towards the city gates. Then, the gates open and a group of soldiers appear, followed by a crowd. In the midst of the soldiers we see the young man from the previous day. He is dressed in a long robe. On his head, he is wearing a strange hat or crown that seems to be made of some form of vegetation and he is carrying a cross on his shoulders. It is obviously too heavy for him, because his gait is uncertain and stumbling. The crowd and the soldiers are jeering and mocking the young man.

My master is silent with the shock of what he is seeing. Without hesitating, he unties me from my post and approaches the soldiers. After some conversation, he lifts the cross from the young man's shoulders. He also finds the cross very heavy. So, he rests one end of the cross on my back and he holds onto the other end. Following the soldiers, we carry the cross. After a while, we leave the road and convey the cross up a steep hill.

When we reach the top of the hill, we stop and lower the cross to the ground. My master and I turn around and make our way back down the hill. We know what is going to happen and we do not want to see. We are familiar with crucifixions. He is very sad. The tears run unashamedly down his face. I am also gripped by a great sadness.

****

I am back on the farm, but my dream is still with me. I know that I have met one of my ancestors from a long time ago. I now understand why mules and donkeys always appear to be so sad. Have you ever heard the call of a donkey? His call is a long, drawn out cry, full of grief and sadness. If we mules could call, we would sound the same.

But, look! Something strange is happening! I can see myself in the paddock! I am high in the sky! And, look! Nelson is standing next to me! I am lying down and Nelson is nudging me!

The dark night is still with us. I look up and see the bright stars. It is as if they are calling to me. I feel young and full of life once more and I instinctively know that I have to answer the call of the stars. But, I also know that I will have to say goodbye to Nelson and all I used to know.

I look up again and I notice that one of the stars is brighter than all the others. That is the one I will aim for. I look at Nelson for the last time.

'Goodbye, Nelson! Take care of yourself.'

And, you know? I think Nelson is aware of what is happening. His thoughts are coming to me as if he is voicing them aloud.

'Goodbye, Dilly, by dearest friend and brother. I will miss you very much, but do not worry unduly. I won't be here for much longer and then I will join you. I am certain that I will know where to find you. Go in peace and be happy.'

I look at him, the paddock and the house for the last time.

'Goodbye, Nelson! Please, be good. Behave yourself. Be nice to Louis and Ezra and Rachael. See you soon!'

I turn round, focus on the bright star and speed on my way.

****

See the rooster.

Apart from his size, he is nothing much to look at. He is not colourful, with long tale-feathers and brightly coloured wings and plumage. And, oh dear! Just look at his pitiful wings! They are short and stubby and useless for flight. All he achieves when he tries to fly is to stir up the dust below him. As a bird he is rather pitiful. He is aptly named: He is quite fowl.

But, be careful. Don't let his outward appearance deceive you. Just look at him! He struts about as if he is king of his domain and in a way he is right. He has the run of the back-yard. No-one disturbs him here.

And look! Just look at his wives! There must be at least ten of them. Quietly crooning, they stroll about, gently grazing on seeds and worms. They are quite reminiscent of contented old ladies.

The rooster will not tolerate interference with him or his. And, when he crows, his call is loud and abrasive. At the end of the night, he summons dawn and it obeys his call.

See the rooster.

6. SAM

Ah, ladies and gentlemen! And, how are you all on this beautiful day? All well? I am glad to hear it. Welcome to this little tour. I am indeed privileged and honoured to be your guide. Now, you want to hear about this magnificent farm of mine? Good! Then sit yourselves down and I will do my utmost to satisfy your curiosity.

You are no doubt wondering why I call this farm, 'mine'. Now there is one thing we have to get quite clear from the start. Since you ladies and gentleman are human, you may very well take sides with the humans who live here and sympathise with them, but let me try and explain. You may, possibly, understand my point of view. This is how I see it:

We, animals have been here much longer than the humans and, as I am sure you know, we birds have been here longer than most creatures. Eventually the creator of animals made some humans and placed them with us and there was a very good reason for this. The creator realised that we, the nobility of the veldt, should not have to slave away and struggle to feed ourselves. So, he created humans and left them here to be our servants. As I see it, they need us as much as we need them. In fact, I would go so far as to say that they need us more than we need them. So, without our help, they could not be farmers. For instance, they specifically like the eggs that my wives produce and when I do my, er, duties, to my wives, the humans are even more pleased, because then they get more birds from the eggs. So, you see, they can hardly survive without us. So, do you understand why I believe that this farm really belongs to me? The humans obviously suffer from a delusion. Poor things!

Now, just step this way and I will give you a bit of a guided tour.

If you look over to your left, you will see a door which is made of wood and fine wire mesh. This door is the entrance to the kitchen. So, this area where we are standing is the kitchen yard. Just to the right of where we stand, there are two big mulberry trees. These provide shade all day long. My wives and I spend most of the day here in this yard. Apart from the shade, there are plenty of worms here and, whenever one of our servants has bits of food, they throw it out here for us.

Now if you would like to follow me, I will show you our living quarters.

As you can see, the humans do try their best to make us comfortable. They have constructed this big, wire cage home for us. Let us go inside and have a look.

Take note, they have constructed perches halfway up the walls of the cage. This is where we sleep at night. There are also some water bowls which are always filled with fresh drinking water.

Now, you are probably wondering why we need to sleep in these cages. Let me explain:

Every evening, just before it gets dark, we come into the cage and one of the servants would come and shut the door. You see, there are some dangerous savages, such as jackals, wild dogs and wild cats around here at night. So, since we are so valuable, the humans have to lock us in here for our protection.

Everyone ok? Good. Now, come with me and I will show you where the horses and the mule live. Do you see that paddock over there? A grassy field enclosed by a steel-wire fence. Do you see the big gray mare? That is Bella. A very nice lady is Bella. She really has very good breeding. I believe that she comes from good Arabian stock.

Now, the young stallion standing next to her is a totally different matter. His name is Nelson and if you ask for my opinion, I think he is a bit common. It is hard to believe that he is the lady's son! Unlike Bella, he has no manners. He is rude and offensive. In other words, I think he is a big, fat, rude oaf with no class.

The stout little animal next to them is Dilly. He is a mule. He is ok, no threat to anyone. Sometimes I have a feeling that he is much brighter than he appears.

Ah! What have we here? See the two creatures coming this way? They are the game hounds, Bruno and Bismark. They are very useful to the humans. Whenever there is hunting or herding to be done, they are called on to help. But, oh my soul! Can they make a racket! You should hear them at night when the moon is full and bright! They howl and bark incessantly! Self-respecting animals hardly get a wink of sleep on these occasions.

Now, let me introduce you to the family:

The man you see sitting over there in the shade, is Mr Danie Le Roux. He is the head servant on my farm. He tells everybody else on the farm what they should be doing. He is having his midday rest. He is pretending to be reading his book, but as you can see, his eyes are tightly shut and he is breathing slowly and very noisily.

Can you see the female servant who is sitting on the stoep *20? She is Mrs Maria Le Roux. She is the mate of the male servant and she is in control of the house. At the moment she is doing some sewing. To tell the truth, I believe that she is really in charge around here. When she says jump, all the other servants jump without asking questions.

And, here come Louis and Bess. They are the offspring of the adult servants. They are not here all the time, but when they are on the farm, they receive lessons from there seniors in the art of being good servants to the animals.

Finally, meet Ezra and Rachael. Rachael helps Mrs Le Roux in the house. She helps with all the cooking and cleaning and scolding of wayward human young. She is also known as regular provider of succulent scraps of food for the farm-yard animals.

Ezra helps Mr Le Roux on the farm. He is by far the cleverest of all of the humans! He understands the farm creatures better than anyone else. We cannot ask for a better servant than Ezra.

So, ladies and gentlemen! We have come to the end of our short tour of the farmyard. I hope you have found it instructive.

What am I going to do now? Oh, I have to go and see to my many wives. They have so many needs, you know. I am constantly expected to see to them. Never mind! As Mr Le Roux quite often says: A man's got to do, what a man's got to do!

Bye, all! See you all soon!

****

See time:

Here, in this part of Africa, time is not judged, or calculated by clock faces and watch mechanisms. Rather, it is expressed as local, natural situations, or everyday events. A local African nature clock will run thus: First crow of the cock, second crow of the cock, third crow of the cock, dawn, milking time, sunrise, breakfast time, morning labour time, noon, lunch time, siesta time, late afternoon labour time, early evening, supper time, sunset, talk time, bed time, night. Chronologically, these are just as real and accurate as time dictated by mechanical clocks.

Imagine the motion of time in different areas of the world, in different situations. In the hustle and bustle of a big city, time fairly races along at Olympic speeds; In a small country town, time lopes along at a fairly jaunty pace; But, here on this African farm, time takes a slow, leisurely walk through the day. Sometimes it nearly stops. Hand in hand, time and its parallel events walk like close friends, through this landscape, sometimes slowing as if to pick a berry or two, sometimes stooping to smell the flowers and sometimes resting so as to listen to the song of the earth.

Time here is as real and inevitable as anywhere in the universe, but it is as personal, benign and benevolent as its companion, the magic of Africa.

See time.

7. TIME

I. DAWN

It is night. It is that time, just before dawn, when all of creation is suspended in a vacuum between mysteries. Behind us, the mystery of the dark, foreboding soul of Africa; the mysterious soul which is proffered, but always snatched back from man's grasp so it may float in ethereal grace, just beyond a vision of complete comprehension. Before us, the mystery of the day. An enigmatic day, which will pose a question, but will keep the answer safely locked in its light. We will observe its long, steady progress of sameness with detached interest and at the end we will say to ourselves:

'Did anything change? Did we achieve anything of substance today which was different from yesterday? Does tomorrow promise a brand new beginning?'

And, the answer will come with a snigger; 'No! Nothing has changed and your achievements have been miniscule.'

But, somewhere, a long way back, in the dim, darkness of man's existence, a single note will sound, like the gentle sound of a single harp string. It is the sound of hope; It is the sound of life; But, most of all, it is the sound of optimistic existence.

Slowly, the moon folds its hands across its face, rubs its tired eyes and prepares to retire for the day. A lone dog, which had kept up an incessant conversation through the night with the moon, falls silent. A dark shadow crosses the farm-yard and the adjoining fields, dimming the light from a million stars.

What is this? A cloud? But, no! It cannot be! The ancients did not see rain in their signs for this day. A flock of birds? Or, could it be the spirits of the dead, but not departed? Those guardians of the secrets of this dark, magnificent continent? And, what is that sound? Is it a roll of thunder in the distance, or the far-off beat of a drum?

Then, as sudden as it came, the shadow is gone and the air clears. All is still.

The old cock crows for the first time. Without awakening, he stretches his long neck forth and releases his four-note melody into the night. The sound pierces the dark and floats away on the clear air. By this means it is carried for some miles, eventually to fade away and to be absorbed on a dew soaked landscape. He does not need to wake to recognise the coming of dawn. His melody is drawn from millions of years of ancestry. Just listen to his song:

'Kukurukuuu! Kukurukuuu! Kukurukuuu!'

The first 3 notes are rhythmic, rapid, stuttering, a building up to the fourth, which is held long and high and in sustained triumph, sliding down to eventually come to rest in a mournful, satisfied sigh of completeness. After a prolonged interval, his song is repeated.

The night remains. Steadfastly, it clings to its dark domain.

But, look now! What is this? The outer edge of darkness is tinted red. The night is faltering. Dawn is coming. The first rays of the sun strikes the top of the trees, revealing them in their dewy, jewel-bedecked splendour of garlands of diamonds, rubies and garnets.

This sight will last for far too short a time. Within minutes, the first heat of the sun's rays will burn away their dewy jewels, exposing them as gnarled, stark survivors, who have to dig deep in order to cling onto an existence in the harsh landscape of the dry veldt.

The cock crows for the third time, but now the message of his song is clear. It is a song of denial of the night and hope of the new day. It says:

'Oh, Darkness. Thank you for your peace. Thank you for your comfort. Thank you for cradling us and wrapping us in dreams. But, now your time is done.'

And, then his song says:

'Oh, Day. Come swiftly and bring your light to show us the way. And, if it pleases you, will you bring some excitement to our lives.'

This is the rooster's song of Dawn.

Inside the house, the old man stirs, stretches and yawns. He gets out of bed, dons his oldest pair of khaki trousers and shirt and stamps his feet into his boots. He goes to the kitchen where he lights the big Aga, makes some coffee and prepares himself for his day's labours: Time for milking! Time for digging! Dime for fencing! And, like the trees, time to burrow deep and survive!

Time has passed. Dawn has been. Day is here.

II. DAY

Time moves on. There are no clocks or other timing devices. Its steady progress is indicated by nature and all creatures, (whether man or beast), understanding and abiding by its relentless demands and ancient laws.

The old man leaves the house. He passes the garden on his left. Without any awareness of his thoughts, he takes note of the fruit trees and the garden fence. Tree pruning and fence mending are stored in his subconscious mind as parts of the coming days labour.

He reaches the kraal where he is met by some farm labourers. They all carry raw hide thongs and enamel milk buckets. In the paddock by the side of the kraal, a milling, lowing mass of cows tramps the ground impatiently. It is time for milking. The herd is as keen to have the discomfort of their full udders relieved as the farmers are to complete their task.

She stands in the paddock with head bowed. She is patient and unquestioning. She came to this place without the need to be herded. She knew it was time for milking.

The gate to the kraal is opened and she enters. She follows one of the farm labourers. He tethers her hind legs and places the bucket below her udder. Rhythmically, he squeezes the teats and pulls down, squirting the foaming milk into the bucket. Only three teats are milked. The fourth is left for her calf. The sweet aroma of hot milk fills the air.

And so, milk time stays for a while, progresses and moves on, giving way to breakfast time.

The old man makes his way back to the house. He enters the kitchen where breakfast of steak, eggs and strong, sweet coffee is waiting. He has already been active for four hours or more and he is hungry. He eats his food with gusto.

And, now it is midmorning. He looks at the sun and knows that the time has come for fencing, ploughing, harvesting and baling.

The sun moves on relentlessly, dragging time behind it. It follows the morning labours. Eventually, it stations itself over the centre of the day. Here it sits like a big, fat ball, grinning its hot grin and daring all living creatures to defy its heat. The shade of the house and the trees beckon and man and beast seek its shelter and protection. It is time for afternoon rest.

After a while, the sun relents. The old man leaves the house and enters the shade of the garden. Here he prunes and waters the fruit trees and the vines.

And so, time walks into the late afternoon. As the sun rolls along to the horizon, the live-stock approaches the dam and the trough. The day has left them parched. The old man fills the trough and the animals drink thirstily.

The end of the day is approaching. After the cattle have quenched their thirst, the old man makes his way back to the house. He joins the woman and the child on the lawn. The woman is slicing runner beans into an enamel bowl. Their conversation is slow and desultory. The child is listening. He is the subject of their discussion. They are talking of sending him away. They say it is for his own good. He needs to go to school. It is a long way from the farm. The old man draws a map of the journey in the dust.

The woman enters the house and after some time the odour of cooking food fills the air. The old man and the child remain on the lawn. They listen to the end of the day.

In the distance, two African farm labourers can be heard chatting to each other as they make their way home for the evening. One of them gives a high, joyful laugh. It is that laugh which is so absolutely unique to the African and his continent. From the direction of the dam a cow moos: "Wait for me! I want to come with you! Let's go back to the field and chew the cud for a while!!"

These sounds travel through the air and settle themselves on the early evening where they join with all those other sounds and become part of the soul of a late African day.

And so, time makes its steady progress. Above the treetops the sun smiles impishly: "Goodbye! Tomorrow is another day, I will be back! Just wait for me!"

Time moves on. Dusk is near. Day is done.

III. DUSK

Dusk is here. It does not stay for long, but in the short time it spends with us, it talks of peace and meditation. The mood of time has become languorous and inactive. It is dragging its tired feet.

Dusk is a most pleasant time period. The heat of the day has gone, but the air is still warm; the great glare of the sun's light has left and the evening light soothes the senses; the race through the day is done and the stroll through dusk is underway.

Dusk does not arrive unexpectedly. It is signalled by the setting sun and the evening chorus of songbirds in the orange trees. Its arrival had been expected and anticipated. Although the sun has left for the day, it is still light. Within minutes the evening chorus changes its tune. The vociferous smaller birds fall silent. Only the wood pigeons can be heard now. Their voices are soft and fragile in the evening air. I am certain that they are talking about friendship, love, courtship and romance.

The woman joins the child and the old man on the lawn. She is carrying a water melon on a tray. The old man takes it from her; from his pocket he produces a pocket knife with which he carves the water melon into slices. Some time of succulent, juicy, indulgence ensues.

The woman re-enters the house and returns after a while with the evening meal, consisting of pumpkin, barley and a beef stew. They eat in companionable silence.

Then, quietly and stealthily, time slips by. At first, the wood pigeons become reflective and then their talk ceases altogether. The air is still; the evening is still; the souls of all the living are still. Then, a lone cricket gives a tentative little croak. He gains confidence and his little chatter becomes more insistent. Then, he is joined by another and still another until the cricket chorus fills the night air. It does not take long before they are joined by some other night sounds. First, a night-owl gives a piercing screech. If you listen carefully, you can hear the radar bleeps of the bats in the orchard. In the distance, where the farm labourers live, someone calls out and a dog barks a response.

The old man, the woman and the child enter the house. It is time to prepare themselves for the night and the long day ahead.

Time has passed. Dusk is done. The dark is here.

IV. DARK

The child lies in his bed. He listens to the night. He hears the voices of the night and he knows them all. He knows instinctively that the sounds of the dark are as ancient, unchanging and permanent as this continent. Since the arrival of humanity and its inventions, new sounds have filled the days of this part of Africa. But, when man retires for the night and the dark arrives, it brings with it millions of years of sameness and magical, uniform certainty.

Gradually, nearly unnoticed, the night grows quiet. One by one the crickets cease their relentless croaking chatter. The child listens to the silence. He knows that this is just a brief interval in a symphony called, Darkness. The noise of the crickets was like a prelude in the concert of time.

The sound of the distant jackal, calling for its mate, opens the next movement of this concert called Darkness. The jackal's call does not shatter the quiet. Instead, it insinuates itself into the night. A night-owl screeches and somewhere on the farm a dog howls at the moon. In the distance, a wild dog gives a high pitched bark. The child listens to the symphony of the night and peacefully drifts into sleep. The night and the dark continue without his attention.

While the time-symphony continues outside, the spirit of the house and the ghost creeps through the rooms. In the bedroom they bring peace to the slumbering occupants. They pass through the rest of the house, and wherever they go, they leave an infusion of peace in their wake.

All is still. All is tranquil and dark. Time moves on.

Gradually the music of the dark begins to fade. The jackal falls silent, the lone dog says goodbye to the moon and the night-owl goes in search of somewhere to hide from the coming day. Like a trumpet call, the cry of the cockerel signals the finale to the music and heralds the arrival of Dawn.

Inside the house, the old man stirs, stretches and yawns. He gets out of bed, dons his oldest pair of khaki trousers and shirt and stamps his feet into his boots. He goes to the kitchen where he lights the big Aga, makes some coffee and prepares himself for his day's labours.

Time for milking, time for digging, time for fencing and, like the trees, time to burrow deep and survive.

Time has passed. Dark has been. Dawn is here. The circle is complete.

****

Hear the voices.

There is a voice of the land. It tells its tales through its creatures, its grass, its trees and its stones. Sometimes its voice can be like a thunder-storm, but mostly it is as gentle as a light breeze. Sometimes the tales are harsh and brutal, but often they are as peaceful as a quiet thought.

The birds tell of their past; of the millions of years before they were birds as we know them now. They tell of riding the air-currents and the leagues and the lands they left behind. They sing of swooping down from great heights and they tell of skimming the surfaces of watery swamps and rivers. And, the eagle tells his tales of how he reigned over all other creatures. In his royal mind, he still does.

The wild animals tell of the time when they owned the veldt. The lion grunts his way through tales of hunting and afternoon slumbers. The hyena laughs about a joke he once heard, although he cannot now remember what it was about. The jackal cries mournfully for the world he had lost and left behind in the dim and distant past.

The tame creatures tell of a time when they ran wild. The pigs tell of their distant cousins, the warthogs, porcupines, aardvarks and wild boar. The cattle and the sheep tell of a time when the sole purpose of their existence was not to be fodder for man.

And, Man? Man tells of that which was passed down by his ancestors. He will also create myths where none exist, because he is the only creature that will lie to justify his existence on the land. Not only will he pass on his stories by word of mouth. He will also tell tales through his dancing.

See the dance.

The women folk sit by the fire and sing their songs. They clap their hands to maintain the rhythm of their song. Their singing is high, ululating and strangely harmonic.

The men-folk dance around the fire. Around their calves they wear strips of seedpods which rattle rhythmically with the dance.

The dance is an expression of man's culture. It tells of the close relationship between animal and man. It tells of the meat which sustains them; It tells of the skins which are used for whips, clothing and, occasionally for food; It tells of the shells of the ostrich eggs which are used for carrying water, or broken and turned into jewellery; It tells of the bones which are used as weapons and digging tools; Sometimes the dance tells of healing and sometimes the dance ask the gods for rain and food.

See the San *25.

They have been on the African continent for eternity. They are not subject to man or land. They are their own people. They have the soul of Africa, but the image of the orient. Where they come from is beyond history or myth.

Hear the voices. See the dance. See the San.

8. LEGENDS

I. WATER

Now then, little one. It is time for you to go to sleep. So, I will tell you a story to help you to your dreams. Now, listen.

A very long time ago, when the world was young, this country where we live was very different from now. There was no desert or dry scrub land. Instead, the now dry river-beds were flowing fast and deep with clear, cool water. Little springs gurgled from the rocky outcrops and ran into brooks which criss-crossed the green, luscious fields. There were no salt-pans, but instead, myriads of little lakes covered the land. Magnificent creatures of all kinds could be seen splashing and drinking in the rivers and lakes, while a gentle sun shone benignly on the scene below.

Where the dry veldt now exists, crops of tall, green grass covered the earth. As far as the eye could see, there were forests, copses and woods of all sizes. Trees that stretched leafy green high into the sky.

In these forests and these grassy fields and along the riverbanks and among the lakes, lived a most strange and wonderful selection of animals. For instance, the tortoise stood tall on fine legs, its body covered in a sleek suit of armour of golden plates, studded with magnificent gems of all shapes and sizes; The snake wandered gracefully on slender legs through the tall grass; The rhino went about, dressed in his smooth, leather coat, with a golden horn perched on his nose; And, the skunk, that young gentleman, strolled about in his furs, smelling as fragrant as the most beautifully scented spring flowers.

Among all these animals, there was one creature who was more beautiful than all the rest. He walked the land with a light step, or he rode on the back of a creature which stood tall and proud. When he sang his songs, all the world stood still and all the animals listened. When he whistled a melody, the air was filled with note-pictures of springs, flowing gently over smooth pebbles. This creature was man.

Above all sat Father Sun, Mother Moon and their star children. By day, Father Sun shone gently on all. When the rivers ran low, he would send some rain, but not too much. Just enough to replenish the lakes and streams and rivers. He looked after all the plants and the fruit and he made sure that there was always enough for all to eat.

At night, Mother Moon guarded over all with a gentle smile. By her light, she guided them through the forests, accompanied by the twinkling eyes of her star children.

One day, the man-creature was sitting on the riverbank. He was cooling his feet in the stream and he was brushing his long hair so that it glistened in the rays of the sun. Next to him stood his proud riding animal. Suddenly, he heard the sound of wings and when he looked up from his beautifying, he saw the largest bird he had ever seen standing next to him.

'You have to come with me,' said the bird.

'But, I cannot,' said the vain man-creature. 'Can you not see that I am intent on important business? I am the most handsome creature on the veldt and all animals look up to me. I cannot disappoint them. I have to beautify myself.'

'Father Sun wants to talk to you,' said the bird.

'Well,' said the man-creature. 'Tell him that I am busy. I may come and see him tomorrow, maybe the day after tomorrow.'

With that, the bird spread its wings and flew away and the man-creature carried on with his preening and beautifying, while his proud animal chewed idly on the green grass.

He was still sitting on the riverbank by the middle of the afternoon when, suddenly, he heard a great roar of wings and he was surrounded by a whirling dust. He looked up in alarm and he saw the giant bird hovering above him.

'Father Sun wants to see you right now!' cried the bird. 'He will not be disobeyed!'

And, with that, he intertwined his long talons in the man-creatures beautiful hair and dragged him into the sky. The man-creature screeched in agony, but the bird paid him no heed. Higher and higher they flew, while the man-creature screamed and struggled with all his might. On and on they flew, for all of that day and all through the night until they reached the sun palace, where the bird dropped the man unceremoniously at Father Sun's feet.

'So, you are the man-creature who would not listen to my command?' asked Father Sun.

'I am sorry, Your Highness,' said the man. 'I did not realise that it was a command. I must have misunderstood.' The man-creature was whimpering on his knees.

'Ha!' snorted Father Sun. 'Be that as it may. I have something that I want you to do for me. I want you to travel to the north veldt where you will find a hill that stands higher than all the other hills. In the side of this hill, you will find a cave and inside the cave, there is a sacred spring. Bring some of the sacred liquid from the spring to me. Looking after you lot is hot and thirsty work. Go now. The bird will return you to the veldt. And, by the way, do not drink any of the liquid. It will do you no good.'

'As long as he does not carry me by my hair!' wailed the man-creature. 'I have such a terrible headache!'

'Hold onto my talons and I will carry you down,' croaked the bird. 'But, mind you don't let go. It is a long way to fall down to earth.'

So, the man-creature clung onto the bird's talons and he was carried back down to the veldt. The bird lowered him gently onto the riverbank from where he had been snatched.

'Why did you not try to save me when that foul bird grabbed me?' shouted the man to his riding animal. 'You will never know how much I suffered! I could have been killed!'

Actually, the man-creature was more concerned with the physical indignity which he suffered.

'Oh. I am sorry,' said the proud animal. 'I did not realise that you had been away. It is just so lovely here and the food is too scrumptious for words!'

'Ha!' said the man-creature. 'You lazy, good-for-nothing! Now we have to go to the north on an errand for Father Sun. And, mind you don't carry me under some low-hanging branches. That confounded bird has pulled half my hair out already.'

So, the man-creature jumped on the proud animal's back and they travelled to the north veldt where they eventually found the hill which stood higher than all the other hills. On the side of the hill, they found a cave and inside the cave, they found the sacred spring. The man-creature filled some water-bags with sacred liquid.

'This smells absolutely delicious!' said the proud animal. 'Why do we not have just a little taste?'

'We are not allowed to,' said the man.

'Who said so?'

'Father Sun,' replied the man.

'Can you see any sign of Father Sun in this cave?' asked the animal. 'If we can't see him, he can't see us. It's so dark in here. If it was not for the moon, shining into the entrance of the cave, I would hardly be able to see a hoof in front of my eyes.'

'You are right,' replied the man-creature. 'Let us just have a little taste.'

So, they went down on their knees and they drank some of the sacred liquid and it was the best thing they had ever tasted.

'This is wonderful!' exclaimed the man-creature. 'I think it is rather selfish of Father Sun to keep it all to himself! We will take this to him and then we will come back and have some more of this liquid for ourselves.'

And, saying this, he jumped onto the proud animal's back and they rode back to the south.

Because night had fallen, they had to travel very carefully. All they had to guide them was the light of the moon. Suddenly, they heard a noise in the bushes.

'Who is there?' called the man-creature.

'It is I,' said a voice and out stepped rhino, his golden horn glinting in the moonlight. 'Where are you going?'

'We are on an errand for Father Sun. We had to collect something in the north for him and we are now returning to the south.'

'What do you carry in those water bags?' asked rhino.

'Some very special sacred liquid,' replied the man.

'Let's have a taste, then,' said rhino.

'No!' said the man. 'We are not allowed to drink this liquid. It belongs to Father Sun, Mother Moon and their children.' But, since he had tasted the liquid already, he was slightly tempted to share it with rhino. 'Why don't you travel with us to the south?'

So, rhino fell into step next to them and they all travelled together.

After another hour's journey, they heard another sound in the bushes.

'Who is skulking there in the bushes?' shouted the man-creature.

'I beg your pardon?' called a voice indignantly. 'Gentlemen do not skulk and I will let you know that I am a proper gent.' And, out stepped Skunk, smelling of spring flowers. 'What are you carrying in those water bags?'

'Not that it is any of your business,' said the man, 'But, since you ask, it is sacred liquid for Father Sun, Mother Moon and their children,' he replied.

'Let's have a taste, then,' said Skunk. 'Nobody will see us.'

'No! Definitely not!' replied the man-creature, but he was sorely tempted. 'Why don't you accompany us on our journey to the south?'

So, the man-creature, his proud animal, Rhino and Skunk continued their journey through the night. Suddenly, they heard another sound in the bushes.

'Who is there?' called the man-creature.

"It is I!' replied a booming voice and out stepped Tortoise, his gold-plated and bejewelled studded armour gleaming in the starlight. 'What are you carrying in those water bags?'

'It is some sacred liquid for Father Sun, Mother Moon and their children,' replied the man-creature.

'May we taste some of this liquid?' asked Tortoise.

"No! We may not!' replied the man-creature angrily. He was very thirsty by now and he was becoming irritable with all these animals trying to tempt him. 'Why don't you just keep quiet about this liquid and travel with us to the south?'

So, the man-creature, his proud animal, Rhino, Skunk and Tortoise continued with their journey through the night until, once again, they heard a sound in the bushes.

'Who is there?' called the man-creature.

'It is I,' replied a silky voice from the dark and, out stepped Snake on long, slender legs. 'Where are you going and what are you carrying in those water bags?'

'It is some sacred liquid for Father Sun, Mother Moon and their children and, before you ask! No! You cannot taste any of it!'

The man-creature was beginning to be very thirsty and he was getting very bad tempered. 'Why don't you all just keep quiet about waterbags! Let us all go south together. If we travel fast, we will reach the river by sunrise and we can all drink water to our hearts content.'

As they travelled through the night, they became thirstier and thirstier. The fact that they could hear the liquid sloshing in the bags didn't help. Eventually they came to a clearing and decided to rest.

'Uhu,' Tortoise cleared his throat. 'I must say, I am really very thirsty. Do you chaps not think that Father Sun is rather unreasonable to deny us some of his liquid? I mean. Just think about it. Here we are, travelling all night long on an errand for him, getting ourselves scratched to pieces on all these thorn-bushes and we can't even have a little sip of his precious liquid. If you ask me, it is totally outrageous!'

'Well. I'm not asking you,' replied the man and they sat in uncomfortable silence for a while. The urge to fidget was impossible to resist and he sighed, scratched himself and picked his nose. Then he said:

'I suppose you have a point. What has Father Sun ever done for us that is so wonderful?'

'He does bring us rain when we need it,' said the proud animal.

'Of course he brings us rain, you stupid animal!' shouted the man-creature. 'But, apart from bringing us rain, what has he ever done for us?'

'He makes the flowers grow,' said Skunk.

'Give me strength!' cried the man-creature. 'Apart from bringing rain and making plants grow, what has he ever done for us?'

'He keeps us warm,' said Rhino.

'I do not believe what I am hearing!' shouted the man. 'Apart from bringing us rain, making things grow and keeping us warm, what has he ever done for us?'

"He gives us light during the day,' said Snake.

'You totally moronic creature!' shrieked the man-creature. 'Apart from bringing rain, making the flowers grow, keeping us warm and giving us light during the day, What does he do for us?'

'Nothing much,' said Tortoise.

'That is right,' said the man. 'I agree with all of you. Apart from these few things, Father Sun has done nothing much for us, compared to our hardships. Therefore, I propose, since the four of you suggested it, that each of us should take just a little sip of this liquid.' And, saying this, he took the stopper out of the waterbag and took a large gulp. He passed the bag to the others and they all drank some of the liquid.

'Aaahhh,' sighed Snake. 'This is wonderful.' And, they all agreed.

None of them quite knew how it happened, but very soon all the bags were completely empty.

I am so very tired. I think I'll just have a little sleep and then decide what to do about getting some more of this liquid.' 'Oh dear!' cried the man, as the realisation of his wrongdoing sank in. 'What will I tell Father Sun? Oh, well. Never mind. It can't be such a big deal. With that, he flopped onto his back and drifted into a deep sleep, shortly followed by the rest of the animals.

They were awakened by a fierce wind. They jumped up in alarm and when they looked up; they saw a flock of enormous birds hovering above them. The rays of the morning sun shone dimly through the dust-cloud that was being whipped up by the birds' wings.

With speed, the birds descended on them. The birds grabbed each of them and then flew up, up, towards the sun. They shrieked and shook and shivered and they swore, but to no avail. When they reached the sun, they were thrown into the sun castle at Father Sun's feet.

'You scoundrels!' roared Father Sun. 'How dare you disobey my commands!'

'What – er – what commands?' wailed the man.

'You were supposed to bring me the sacred liquid. You good-for-nothing, idle creatures. You drank it all yourselves! Mother Moon saw it all.'

The man, fearful in the presence of Father Sun, stuttered 'But, it was their fault, Father Sun.' How could he have forgotten the awesome power of Father Sun's presence. 'They said that you did nothing for us and that it would be alright to drink the sacred liquid.'

'Don't lie to me!' shouted Father Sun. 'For what you have done, you will be severely punished.'

He looked at them very sternly and said: 'You, Tortoise, will lose your long legs and your golden armour. I will make you so ugly, that you will hide your head forever in your shell.' And, with that, he threw Tortoise out of the castle and he fell all the way down to earth, where he landed on a rock and he lost his golden armour and his shell became all bumpy.

'And, you, Snake. From now on you will crawl through the grass on your belly and, mind that nobody stamps on your head.' Snake was tossed down to earth.

'And, you, Rhino. You walk about so proud in your fancy coat. That will soon be fixed.' And, with that, Father Sun threw him out of the castle. Rhino landed in a clump of thorny bushes. All the gold was scratched off his beautiful horn and his coat was torn to bits and it became all knobbly and creased. He accidentally looked into a pool of water and his reflexion was so horrid that he became very shy and defended himself quite aggressively.

'Skunk,' said Father Sun. 'From now on I will make sure that all other creatures avoid you.' And, with that, he threw him into a pool of mud, slime and sulphur. From that day on, Skunk lost his beautiful perfume and stank so much, that everybody avoided him.

'Man,' said Father Sun. 'for questioning my powers, I will make you suffer most. I will bring no more rain, I will stop the flowers from growing and I will really make it very hard for all of you. There will be no more forests and green fields and rivers. Instead, I will give you endless sand and dust and scrub land. You will not ride on this proud animal anymore. Instead, you will be forced to wander this barren land on foot, endlessly searching for water and food.'

Finally, Father Sun turned to the proud animal; 'You. You proud animal. Instead of standing proud and tall, you will become small and ugly. You will lose your beautiful voice. From now on, when you talk, you will grunt and squeak. As well as being idle, you will also become stubborn. And, finally, I will give you an ugly name to suit your appearance. From now on, you will be called, donkey.'

And, that, little one, is how this land of ours was created. Now, close your eyes, it's time to sleep.

II. CHEAT

Now, little one. Let me tell you the story of Ostrich and Tortoise and how Tortoise cheated Ostrich. Before I start, I will explain to you about some of their characteristics.

Ostrich is a really big bird with long legs and neck, a small head and scrawny wings. He cannot fly, but he can run quite fast. He is also incredibly stupid. He has the brains of a fly! But, he is very proud of the fact that he can run very fast.

Tortoise lives in a thick shell. He is probably the laziest creature on the veldt. Most of the day he can be found, fast asleep in the shade of a bush with his head and his legs pulled up into his shell. But, unlike Ostrich, Tortoise is a very clever creature. Unfortunately, he is also very conceited and a liar beyond belief.

Both Ostrich and Tortoise lived on the veldt. Ostrich lived in the south and Tortoise lived in the north. There was a time when they did not know each other. There was plenty for them to eat in the different parts of the veldt where they lived, so there was no need for their paths to cross. Unfortunately, one year, the land was visited by a big drought and food and water became very scarce in the south and Ostrich decided to travel to the north to look for food.

So, this is what he did. He travelled to the north and found himself a lovely, bushy area on the veldt where he took shelter. Because he was new to the area, he did not meet any other creatures at first, apart from the birds that lived in the bushes around him.

Now it just so happened that, One day Ostrich was doing a bit of idle grubbing in the sand. He was not really thinking about much at the time. He was just enjoying the sunshine and eating worms and seeds. And then he thought:

'I have not been running lately. I think I may go for a run this afternoon. I don't want to become fat and lazy, do I! I wonder if there is anyone who would like to race with me? Obviously I will beat them, because I am the fastest running bird on the veldt. But, it will be nice to have some competition. I wish I knew somebody else around here;

This thought had just crossed his mind when he heard a voice behind him:

'Good afternoon. Now, just who may you be?'

Ostrich looked behind him for the voice. At first he couldn't see anyone, apart from a thing that looked like a stone to him.

'Who is talking to me?' asked Ostrich. 'Come on! Show yourself!'

'I am talking to you,' said the stone. 'It is tortoise!'

'Oh hello, Tortoise,' said Ostrich. 'I have heard a lot about you, but I have never met you. So, obviously, I didn't recognise you there. How are you? And, by the way, my name is Ostrich.'

'Oh, hello there, Ostrich. I have heard of you. Thank you. I am fine. Very busy as usual,' said Tortoise. How about you? What are you up to these days?'

'Just grubbing and thinking,' replied Ostrich. 'In fact. I was just thinking that I would like to go for a little run.'

'Ah,' said Tortoise. 'What a good idea. There is nothing like a good run! I go for a run every morning. Gives me a good appetite, you know. I raced against Lion this morning. Left him standing in the dust. Didn't have a chance against me!'

'Oh, really?' asked Ostrich. 'Would you consider coming for a run with me? Let's have a race. Oh, please, Tortoise. I would really enjoy it.'

'Uh,' said Tortoise. 'I don't know about that. Very busy, you know. Have to go and visit a sick friend this afternoon. Tomorrow I have to go to the other side of the veldt to visit some family.'

'Let us do it next week, then,' said Ostrich.

Tortoise was now thinking fast. He really should not have boasted like that. He realised that Ostrich was not going to give up.

'Where do you want to run to, and where should we start?'

'Do you see that big hill in the distance?' asked Ostrich. 'I thought we might start here and run to the hill. It will only take a day. O, please, Tortoise! Say you will!'

'Uh, Let us do it at the start of next week, then,' said Tortoise. 'It will give you a few days to practise.'

'Oh, goodie!' said Ostrich. 'I will see you here in four days time.'

Tortoise walked away and went and hid under a bush. He had a lot to think about. What should he do? How could he possibly race against Ostrich? How could he get out of this without being totally humiliated?

'Oh, well,' he thought. 'I have some time before the race and I am certain that I will think of something. I am sure I will find a way out of this situation, since I am the cleverest animal on the veldt.

So, he decided to indulge in his most favourite past-time. He pulled his legs and his head into his shell, closed his eyes and went to sleep.

When he woke up the next day, he still had no idea of what to do. He thought and he thought and he thought, but he just could not come up with a good plan. Another day went by and he realised that he was running out of time.

On the morning of the second day, the beginnings of a plan came into his head. He had to get some help and he knew just where to get it from!

So, he set off to see all his family and friends of whom he had a great number. By the evening he had gathered them all together and he told them about his problem.

'Dear family and friends,' he said. 'This funny old bird called Ostrich, challenged me to a race. He wants to run from here to that big hill in the distance. I obviously told him that I could not run very fast, but he just laughed at me and called me very bad names. He said terrible things about us tortoises. He said that we were all lazy and slow and ugly. So, you see, dear friends. I had no choice but to agree to race against him. I have to do it for the honour of all of us.'

Oh, what a liar! So, this was Tortoise's plan.

'I will be at the starting line with Ostrich. I want you lot to stretch out at intervals in a long line to the finishing point at the hill. Hide under bushes so that Ostrich can't see you, apart from the one who will be waiting for him at the finishing line. I think you should all set off to your places tonight. It is a long way to go.'

So, that is what they did. Tortoise went back to his bush, pulled his head and legs into his shell and went to sleep. He felt really exhausted after the thinking he had to do.

On the third day, he went to look for Ostrich. He found him standing in the shade of a tree.

'Hello there, Ostrich. How are you today? Have you been practising?

'Oh, yes. I have been running a bit.' said Ostrich. 'Are you ready for the race tomorrow?'

'Can't wait! Really looking forward to it!' said Tortoise. 'So, I will meet you here at sunrise.'

'Absolutely,' said Ostrich. 'See you tomorrow morning.'

No need to say, but Tortoise went straight to his bush and went to sleep.

The next morning they bet at the starting point.

'Right,' said Tortoise. 'It is a long way to go. So, I suggest we make an early start. If you are ready, I will count to three and we can be off.'

'Ready when you are,' said Ostrich.

'Right then. One, two, three, go!' shouted Tortoise and they were off, or rather, Ostrich was off. Tortoise yawned, stretched his neck, closed his eyes and went to sleep once more.

Ostrich ran and ran and ran with all his might. Every now and then he would call out: 'Tortoise! Where are you?' and the voice of tortoise would come: 'I am right behind you! Run faster, Ostrich! I am right behind you!'

Poor old Ostrich. What a trick to play on him. All day he ran and ran and whenever he called for Tortoise, that voice of Tortoise was right behind him.

Eventually, in the late afternoon, he reached the hill. Just imagine his astonishment when he saw Tortoise lying there, fast asleep as usual.

'Tortoise!' shouted Ostrich. 'I thought you were behind me! When did you get here?'

Tortoise yawned and stretched his neck. 'Oh, hello Ostrich. Where have you been for so long? I have been waiting for you. Must have dozed off. I have been here for some time. I overtook you some distance back. I was running so fast that you did not see me passing you. I was just having a nap whilst waiting for you.'

So, that is how Tortoise won a race against Ostrich. What a cheat!

Now, it is time for you to go to sleep, little one.

III. HARE

In the last story we established that Tortoise was probably the cleverest creature on the veldt, but he was also the laziest. The next story is about Hare, Elephant and Hippo and how Hare managed to fool Elephant and Hippo. Well, it just so happened that Tortoise was having a sleep one day under his normal bush. His head and his legs were firmly hidden. Suddenly, he woke up. Someone was knocking on his shell.

'Who is there?' he yawned. 'Who is disturbing me in the middle of the night?'

'It is not the middle of the night, you lazy old fool!' called a voice. Stick your head out of your shell! I want to talk to you! I need your help!'

Tortoise yawned, stretched his neck and opened one eye. It was a bright, sunny day and there, next to him, stood Hare.

'Hello there, Hare!' said Tortoise. 'And, how are you today?'

'I am fine, thank you,' said Hare. 'I am just having a few problems with Elephant and Hippo and I have come here to see you. I am hoping that you might be able to help me.'

'Sit down, old chap,' said Tortoise. 'Come. Tell me what the problem is.'

Let me just say something about Tortoise before we continue: Tortoise has many qualities, some good and some not so good. For example, he is a cheat, he is lazy, but he is also very clever and he can be very generous and helpful to others.

Anyway, Hare sat down and told him what the problem was:

'They always take the Mickey out of me,' said Hare. 'They laugh at me and they call me weak and feeble. The other day, Elephant just came along and picked me up with his trunk. He put me up on one of the highest branches of the tree. You would not believe the difficulties I had trying to come down. I had to hide in the leaves from all the birds of prey. If it was not for the help I had from a group of passing monkeys, I would probably still be up there.

'And, then there is the problem with Hippo: He also mocks me and he bullies me all the time. A few days ago I was sitting on the riverbank, minding my own business. Hippo sneaked up behind me, picked me up in his mouth and threw me into the deepest part of the river. Now, if there is one thing that hares can't do, it is swimming. Luckily for me a log came floating by and I managed to cling on to it. I floated in the river until I got near to the riverbank in the shallows before I managed to jump out of the water onto dry land. I was many miles away from home and it took me nearly a day to get back home.'

'Yes. I see what you mean,' said Tortoise. 'That is really bad. We cannot allow this to continue. We will have to see what could be done about it. Leave it with me for a day or so.

Come and see me again the day after tomorrow. I will think of a plan by then.'

'Thank you very much, Tortoise. I will see you the day after tomorrow, then.' And off he hopped.

For the rest of that day, Tortoise thought and thought. By the evening an idea came into his head and by the next morning he had worked out a plan.

'Have you thought of a plan, Tortoise?' asked Hare.

'Oh, yes,' said Tortoise. 'But, we are going to need a lot of help. Have you many brothers and sisters and other family?'

'Oh, yes,' said Hare.

'Good,' said Tortoise. 'I want you and your family to go and dig out as many wild cucumber creepers*21 as you can find. Then, I want you to take all the plants onto the big empty plain on the other side of the bush land. I will meet you there in two days time.'

So, that is what Hare did. He collected all his family together and all the next day they dug out the wild cucumber creepers and the following morning they took all of these to the big plain where they met Tortoise.

Now, let me tell you about wild cucumber creepers. These grow along the ground. The wild cucumbers are round and juicy, but with very spikey skins. However, the creepers themselves are extremely tough.

'Now,' said Tortoise, 'I want you lot to weave all these creepers together so that we can create a very long, strong rope. All the hares, being very nimble animals, did as they were told. They intertwined the creepers and, in no time at all, they had the longest, strongest rope on the plain.

Once the rope was made, Tortoise told Hare what to do next.

The following day Hare went looking for elephant. Eventually he found him. He was picking fruit from the high branches of a tree.

'Hello, Elephant!' cried Hare. 'May I have a word with you?'

'Now, what could you possibly have to say to me, you feeble little animal.'

'I want to challenge you to a contest,' replied Hare.

'What kind of a contest?' asked Elephant.

'A trial of strength,' replied Hare.

'A trial of strength!' cried Elephant. 'What on earth are you talking about. What a laugh! But, tell me. I am very interested.'

'Right,' said Hare. 'This is the plan. My family and I have created a rope from wild cucumber creepers. We have left it on the open plain. I want you to pick up one end of the rope and I will do the same at the other end. We will then pull against each other. If you should beat me, then you can do whatever you like with me. But, if I should beat you, you must never treat me badly again and you should show me respect.'

'Right,' said Elephant. 'So it shall be. When will this contest be?'

'I will meet you there in the early morning, just before sunrise of the day after tomorrow,' said Hare. Elephant agreed to this and Hare went off to find Hippo.

He found Hippo the next day down by the river.

'Hello, Hippo! How are you?' asked Hare.

'What has it to do with you?' asked Hippo.

'I would like to challenge you to a contest,' Replied Hare.

'What! You want to challenge me? What could you possibly beat me at?' asked Hippo.

'Let me tell you,' replied Hare. 'My family and I have made a rope out of wild cucumber creepers. It is really think and strong. We have left it out on the big plain. I want you to meet me there. I would like you to pick up one end of the rope and I will do the same with the other end. We will then pull against each other. If you beat me, you can do whatever you want to me, but if I beat you, you will have to treat me as an equal from now on. How about it?'

Hippo laughed and laughed until the tears were streaming from his eyes.

'Alright,' he said when he eventually gained control of himself. 'So, when shall we do this?'

'How about early tomorrow morning?' asked Hare. 'I will meet you just after sunrise.'

'If you wish,' said Hippo. 'See you there.'

So, the next morning Hare arrived on the battle-field nice and early. Just before sunrise, Elephant arrived.

'Let me take you to the end of the rope,' said Hare. 'We will have our battle when the sun is up.'

Hare ran back very quickly to meet Hippo, who arrived just after sunrise.

'Come with me,' said Hare. 'I will take you to the end of the rope. Then, when you are in position, I will walk to my end and the battle can start. Is that alright with you?'

'Oh, certainly, little weasel,' said Hippo and sniggered.

This, then, was what Hare did. Because both animals did not have very good sight, they did not see each other.

Hare walked to the middle of the rope and picked it up. Elephant could see Hare and Hippo could see Hare, but Elephant and Hippo could not see each other.

'Right! Are you ready? Then pull!' Shouted Hare and Elephant and Hippo pulled with all their might.

It was absolute mayhem. Elephant would gain a few inches and then Hippo would gain a bit. But, all in all it was stalemate. The contest went on for hours and hours. No-one was winning.

Eventually Hare had enough. He picked up a very sharp stone and with a quick slash of the sharp end, he cut the rope. Elephant went flying and landed on his back. Hippo staggered back and fell down, quite exhausted. Hare walked over to him and said:

'So. Have you had enough?'

'Yes! Oh, yes!' groaned Hippo.

'Will you treat me with respect from now on?'

'Oh, yes. I will,' said Hippo.

'Then, get up and run back to the river before I change my mind and give you a good thrashing!'

Hippo jumped to his feet and staggered back to the river.

Then, Hare walked to Elephant and said:

'Right! You big fat oaf! Have you had enough of the contest, or would you like us to continue?'

'Please! No more!' groaned Elephant.

'Will you treat me with respect from now on?' asked Hare.

'Oh, yes. I promise,' said Elephant.

'Then get up and go back to your trees! Quick! Before I change my mind,' said Hare.

Elephant staggered to his feet and lumbered off as fast as he could.

It is very likely that Elephant and Hippo found out how they were tricked, but it is unlikely that they would have done anything about it. You see, all the other animals had heard the story and Elephant and Hippo became the laughing stock of the veldt. Hare had suddenly become very popular, so Elephant and Hippo would not have been allowed to take revenge. From that day on, they left him alone and treated him with the utmost respect.

IV. JACKAL

This is the story of Jackal and Hyena. Are you ready little one? Right. Then, we'll begin.

Jackal and Hyena were very good friends. They were neighbours who lived in the same part of the veldt. They hunted together, fed together and played games together. In fact, they spent every free minute of the day in each other's company.

In the part of the veldt where they lived, there was a big pan, filled with fresh water. This meant that there were loads of other animals in the area, because, every evening all the creatures would come to the pan to drink. The surrounding land was also lush and green. All this meant that there was no shortage of anything to eat or drink.

Jackal and Hyena really loved the land. Their lives were most comfortable, they had all the friends they wanted and, most of all Jackal could pursue his hobby. Let me tell you about Jackal's hobby.

You see, Jackal liked to sing. He had a most beautiful voice. He would walk the veldt and sing his heart out while he was strolling in the long grass. Quite often, in the warm evenings, he would sit under the tree where he lived and sing and sing. On many occasions the other animals would come and listen to him and quite often they would join in the singing. Oh, what good, joyful times they had! This was indeed the happiest place on the veldt!

But then, as it is with most things, very little in this life lasts forever. Gradually, without many realising it at first, things started to change. First, the rains did not come as frequently as they did, and then stayed away altogether. The water in the pan dwindled and eventually dried up completely. The land surrounding the pan became arid and infertile. All the animals moved away. You see, they had no choice. They were starving and they had to go and find some food and water.

At first, Jackal and Hyena tried to stay where they were. They believed that the rain could not stay away for good. But, alas, they waited and waited and nothing changed. The fields became drier; the trees lost their leaves which meant that there was very little shade from the sun, which was becoming hotter and hotter by the day. Eventually, they could stand it no longer and they decided to leave.

'But, where shall we go?' asked Jackal. 'I know nowhere else.'

'We will go in search of the man-creatures,' said Hyena. 'We will go and work for him. He will look after us. Surely there will be something we can do for him and he can pay us with food and water.'

So, this is what they did. Day after day they walked across the veldt, looking for signs of the man-creature. Whenever they met other animals, they would ask for news, but for a long time they did not learn anything. And then, one day, they came upon an aardvark on the veldt. He was busy removing ants for his supper from a giant anthill.

'Numm, numm, numm,' said Aardvark. 'Afternoon, Jackal! Afternoon, Hyena! And where have you two sprung from? Goodness me! You look tired and thirsty! Would you like some ants?'

'No, thanks, Aardvark,' said Hyena. 'We do not eat ants. But, you are right. We are thirsty and hungry. We have travelled a long way. The pan where we lived has gone dry and all the animals have left. We are looking for the man-creature. We want to do some work for him so that he can pay us with food and drink. You don't by any chance know where he is?'

'Mm. Let me think,' said Aardvark. 'Now that you mention it, I think I have heard some rumours of his whereabouts. I was told that he lives in the direction from which the sun rises every day. But, it is a long way from here and it may take you some days to reach him.'

'But, how will we know him when we meet him?' asked Jackal.

'Oh. He is very different from all other creatures,' replied Aardvark. 'For a start, he walks on two legs.'

'But, so do monkeys and birds,' said Hyena.

'Ah, but he is not covered in feathers or hair. Also, he dwells in a different place to us. He does not live under ground, or in trees, or in the bushes. He has made himself a dwelling above ground. It is made from mud, clay and animal manure.'

They thanked Aardvark and set off again. Day after day they walked in the direction from which the sun rose. They knew that they were going the right way, because all the animals they met on the way told of the man-creature who lived on the veldt.

One evening jackal suddenly stopped walking. He sniffed the air.

'What is it?' asked Hyena.

'There is a strange smell in the air,' replied Jackal. 'It is the smell of something that lives, but not creatures of the veldt like us.'

'Let us go on and investigate,' said Hyena.

So, that is what they did. Slowly and stealthily they proceeded. Then, they saw a glimmer among the trees. They followed the light until they reached a clearing. Here, at last, they saw the man-creature. They recognised him from the description Aardvark gave them. He was sitting at the entrance to his dwelling from which emanated the light that they had seen.

Jackal was so happy that he burst out in joyful song. The notes were high and clear. He thanked the moon, the stars and the sun for their deliverance from the dry veldt. The man-creature heard his song and came to investigate. When he saw them, he recognised them for what they were: Poor, starving creatures of the veldt.

'Come with me,' called the man-creature.

They followed him into the clearing where he gave them water to drink and food to eat. Then he beckoned them to come and sit by his side.

'Now,' said he. 'Tell me your story.'

And, that is what they did. They told him of life around the watering pan, the lush green veldt, the land of plenty and, then of the drought and their starvation. Then they told him of their search for him.

'We would like to come and perform some tasks for you. In exchange we would like you to feed us.'

'Yes,' said the man-creature. 'That is indeed a possibility. You stay and sleep here for the night. I will think of something for you to do. I will let you know in the morning.'

Early the next day the man-creature came and woke them and said:

'I think I have some work for you. Can you both dig holes?'

'Off course we can,' replied Hyena. 'I am a very good digger.'

'He is right,' said Jackal. 'We both can dig holes. What do you want us to do?'

'Well,' replied the man-creature. 'The entire veldt is dry at the moment. In this part of the veldt we also had very little rain. But, I know that there is lots of good water under the ground. All that is needed is to dig a deep hole and then we will all have enough to drink. If you would dig the hole, I will give you food and drink.'

'Of course we will,' said Hyena. 'We will start straight away.'

Jackal did not say a lot. To tell the truth, he was not a very good digger Remember, he preferred to sit under a tree and sing songs.

Anyway, the man-creature showed them the place where they had to dig for water and told them to start digging.

'Every evening, when you have done a day's digging, come to my dwelling and I will feed you,' he said and left.

'Shall we get started then?' asked Hyena.

'Well,' said Jackal. 'Would you like me to sing you a beautiful song? It is a new song that you have not heard before. I know what we can do. You start digging and I will sit under that tree and sing for you. That will pass the time and make it much easier for you.'

'If you say so,' said Hyena and he started digging.

Jackal settled himself under a tree and sang and sang and Hyena dug and dug. Hyena was so busy digging and he enjoyed the singing so much that he did not notice how swiftly the day went by. When the sun was just about to set, Jackal stopped singing and said:

'Hyena! I think we have done enough for the day. We have really worked very hard. Let's go and see the man-creature and have some well deserved food.'

When they reached the man-creature's dwelling, Hyena looked very tired, but Jackal also pretended to be tired.

'We have really worked very hard today,' said he. 'Can we please have some food and drink?'

So, they were fed and watered and went to sleep.

For many days the same thing happened: Hyena would dig for water and Jackal would sit and sing. Eventually Hyena thought to himself:

'This does not seem right. I am digging all day and Jackal just sits and sings. I know he has a very good voice and the songs are nice, but surely! I am working a lot harder than him. I think I'll have a word with the man-creature.'

That night, when Jackal was asleep, Hyena went to the man-creature and told him all about it.

'All day long I dig and dig and Jackal just sits under the tree and sings. Do you think that is right?'

'No,' replied the man-creature. 'Leave it to me. I will see to the scoundrel.'

The next day was the same as all the other days: Hyena was digging and Jackal was sitting under the tree and singing. In the afternoon, the man-creature crept up behind them and saw what was happening. He was really very cross. He jumped out from behind the bush where he was hiding and shouted:

'You lazy little animal! You have been lying to me! You told me you were working, but all the time you have just been sitting here under the tree, doing nothing!'

Saying this, he slapped jackal very hard and he kicked him and he hurled him into a big bush. Jackal's song changed from a beautiful melody to a high-pitched wail and he ran away as fast as he could.

From that day on, Jackal was very seldom seen during the day on the veldt. He became a creature of the night. You see, he was too worried that the man-creature would spot him and attack him.

His songs also changed. Instead of the beautiful melodies, his songs became mournful. If you are sitting by the fire in the veldt at night, you will hear his call:

'I am so alone! Is there anyone who I will share my sadness?'

And, the reply would come from the other jackals:

'We can hear you! Don't be afraid! We will share the dark with you!'

So, what do you make of this tale? My little one! Was Jackal wrong to sing and not work? Or was he stupid? Should he have been more honest from the beginning? He sneaked off and complained to the man-creature like that! That is not how friends behave. On the other hand, wasn't Jackal a very clever cheat?

But now, when we sit around the camp-fire at night and listen to them calling, don't they sound so very sad? I feel quite sympathetic towards him now, don't you?

V. SUN

A very, very long time ago, when the world was young everything was fresh and new, things were so much different from now. Let me tell you of some of these differences.

One big difference was that there was so much more water than there is now. That meant that the grass was always green and lush and the bushes were covered in ripe berries all the year round. But, the biggest difference of all was in the sky. You see, it may be difficult to understand, but sun did not live up there. Sun lived down here with the creatures of the veldt. Because he was so very young, he was not very hot. So, he just sat in one place and all the animals came to see him. They would talk to him, play games with him and generally just have a lot of fun with him.

Then, one day, things started to change. Sun began to get hotter. At first it happened very slowly, but then, after a while, it happened more rapidly. Eventually things became quite unbearable. Sun would be nice and cool in the morning, but by midday he became unbearably hot. So, eventually the animals did the only thing that was left to them; they deserted sun and went to live in a different part of the veldt.

Now, you have to understand that sun was not bad. He could not help what he was. It was just natural that he should get hotter. There was nothing he could do about it. So, when all the animals left, he was really sad. You see, he really believed that they were all his friends and now they were deserting him.

So, sun just sat there in the veldt. In the mornings he was nice and cool, but as the day progressed, he got hotter and hotter. Eventually, the veldt around him all dried up. The grass and the bushes shrivelled away and the waterholes became empty. Now, under a tree, far away from sun in a different part of the veldt, lived Jackal. He stayed here with his parents and his brothers and sisters. They were a very happy family of animals. They never went far from their home for that was the way of jackals. Instead, they used to play in the long grass and at night they used to sing to the moon and the stars.

One day Jackal said to his parents:

'I have been living here since I was born. I would like to go and see the world. I have heard that the veldt is very big and that there are many strange creatures living in it. So, tomorrow I will go on my way.'

So, that is what he did. The next day he rose early, had some food and water and then he went on his way.

He walked and walked, for day after day. At night he would sleep in the shelter of bushes. On his way he met all kinds of animals, such as leopards, lions, gemsbok, springbok, steenbok *22 and duikers *23.

One day he noticed a change in his surroundings. It was in the middle of the day and he realised that it was getting hotter. He also saw that the grass was not as green as it should be and that the shrubs were very dry. He came to a waterhole and he decided to have a drink, but when he got closer, he saw that it was empty.

'This is all very strange,' he thought to himself. 'I will have to find some shade. It is so very hot.'

After a while he saw a tree. It was very dry and the leaves were brown, but it provided a little shade where he rested for the rest of the day.

In the evening, when it was cooler, he left the tree and continued with his walk. Late that night he saw a big round thing on the ground ahead. As he got closer, the sphere spoke to him:

'Hello, Jackal. Am I glad to see you!'

'Who are you?' asked Jackal.

'I am Sun,' said the ball.

'What are you doing here?' asked Jackal.

'I have been here for a long time,' said Sun.

'Where are all the other creatures and why is it so dry here?' asked Jackal.

'There used to be many animals and birds here. They were all my friends. But, then it became very hot and dry. I really have no idea why that happened,' lied Sun, 'But they all went away and left me here by myself.'

'That is terrible!' cried Jackal. 'Come. You climb onto my back and I will take you away from here. I will take you to my parents' house. They will take care of you.'

Jackal knelt down on the ground and Sun rolled onto his back. All night he carried Sun without resting. The next morning, he noticed that Sun was getting very hot.

'You are too hot!' cried Jackal. 'Can you please get off my back!'

'No,' said Sun. 'I want you to carry me all the way to the other animals, then I will get off your back.'

So, Jackal carried on walking with Sun on his back. By late afternoon, his back was really very sore and he could stand it no longer. In the distance he could see a tree with big roots and low hanging branches. As fast as he could, he ran to the tree. When he got there, he rubbed his back against the bark, he rolled on his back and rubbed against the roots and he rubbed his back against the low branches until Sun lost his grip and fell off. Then he ran as fast as he could, back to his parents' house.

When he got home, he told them how he tried to help Sun but that Sun was hurting him too much so he escaped and ran home. The burns on the young jackal's back were deep and sore, so they took some ashes from a grass fire and mixed it with the juices from plants to make a poultice. This was gently laid on his back to help heal his burns and soothe his skin. And that is why to this day, Jackal still has a white stripe down his back. Doesn't it look like ashes? And what do you think happened to Sun?

When the rest of the animals heard of Sun's bad behaviour, they were very cross. They had an indaba *24 to decide what to do about it. Some thought that he had to be buried and others wanted him to be thrown in to the deepest pan of water. Eventually Elephant spoke: 'Leave it to me. I will take care of Sun.'

When he found Sun where Jackal left him, he said:

'You have caused all of us a lot of trouble. You have caused a lot of the veldt to dry and whither. You have caused a lot of animals to suffer and die. This cannot be allowed. But, most of all, you have been very badly behaved towards Jackal. You lied to him when he was trying to help you and you have caused him severe suffering. I am going to put you somewhere where you can be of benefit to all.'

Saying this, he picked Sun up with his trunk and tossed him as high as he could. Sun flew and flew and flew. He passed the moon and eventually, he reached the stars and it was here that he stopped. Here, in his new home, he was happy and he did many good and kind things. Eventually he grew very large. His heat and rays helped plants to grow and on cold winters days he kept all the creatures warm.

Eventually, when the man-creatures arrived on the veldt, he became one of the gods that they prayed to. They called him Father Sun and the moon they called Mother Moon.

VI. DOVE

This is a little tale about a dove. When the land was young and the birds were first created, this dove was a very vain and proud creature. She thought herself better and prettier than all the other birds. When any birds would dare to approach her, or perch anywhere near her, this little dove would chase them away by saying to them: 'Sit-a-little that-way. Sit-a-little that-way.'

At first the other birds tried their best to make friends with the dove, but she refused steadfastly to be kind to them. As soon as they came near her, she would say: 'Sit-a-little that-way.'

Eventually, the birds had enough of the dove's bad manners and they all decided to leave her alone.

'What a really unpleasant, bad mannered creature,' they all said. 'We have tried very hard to make friends with her, but she does not want to be friends with us, so we will go away and she can live all by herself.'

So, that is what they did. They moved to the other side of the veldt and the little dove was left to fend for herself. At first she really enjoyed herself. She had so much space! She had all the open sky to herself! Oh, what freedom.

Then, one day, a feeling of unease came upon her, but she could not immediately identify what it was. When she woke, she had gone down to the stream where she had a wash. Then she preened her feathers and cleaned her beak and her feet. After that she went for a fly, but something was not right. The veldt around her seemed very empty. There was no life in the branches of the trees at all and she was surrounded by complete silence. So, she perched on a high branch of a tree and called: 'Is-there-anyone-there? Is-there-anyone-there?' but she got no reply.

Gradually she realised what the problem was: She was lonely and afraid.

'What shall I do?' she thought to herself. 'I know! I will go and find the other birds.'

So, that is what she did. She flew and she flew and she searched for the other birds and as she flew, she called out: 'Where-are-you-all-hiding?' And 'don't-stay-away-from-me.'

All day she flew and she searched, but she could not find them. Eventually, exhausted and miserable, she perched in a tree and went to sleep.

Early the next morning she was woken by a familiar sound. Dawn was just around the corner and it was beginning to be light. Then, suddenly, she realised what had woken her. It was the sound of chirping birds! It was the dawn chorus!

Swiftly she flew in the direction of the birdsong. She did not even bother to preen her feathers, or clean her beak and feet.

When she reached the birds, she sat in a tree near them and called quietly: 'Sit-a-little-this-way.'

She called very quietly, because she was worried that they would chase her away. But, she did not have to worry. They all surrounded her and welcomed her with open wings. Because, you see, most birds, apart from birds of prey, are really very kind and gentle.

To this day, if you should stand in the veldt and listen to the birds, you can hear the red-eyed dove calling: 'Sit-a-little-this-way. Sit-a-little-this-way.'

VII. RAIN

This is a little story of Elephant and the weather.

Have you ever seen an elephant in the wild? Have you noticed the appearance of his skin? It is all wrinkly and shrivelled. It looks as if he must be very old.

Have you ever seen an elephant from behind? If you look at a bull-elephant's legs, you can clearly see his testicles hanging down, or rather; you can see one of them. So, let me tell you why Elephant's skin and testicles look like that.

Elephant used to be a very handsome animal. He had the smoothest skin and he displayed all the colours of the rainbow. But, unfortunately, he was not very popular with the other animals. This is the reason why.

You see, Elephant was a very vain creature. He was always telling the other animals about the wonderful things he could do and he never had to prove anything to them. If they should ask him to prove that he could do something, he would just wave them aside with his trunk.

Because he was so much bigger than all the other animals, He was also a bully. He had absolutely no manners! For example, if he should get to a waterhole and it was surrounded by other, smaller creatures, he would simply barge his way to the front. If anyone should have the temerity to oppose him, he would just push them out of the way. Sometimes, just for his own pleasure, he would pick an animal up in his trunk and throw them into the water.

Now, Weather, (who cared very much for the land and who looked after all the animals), had observed Elephant's behaviour and he decided to teach him a lesson. So, he spoke to Rain-drop and he told him of his plan.

One day, Elephant was just standing in the veldt when he noticed that it was beginning to be cloudy. Suddenly he felt a raindrop on his trunk.

'Hello, there, Elephant,' said Raindrop. 'And, how are you today?'

'I am fine, thank you,' said Elephant. 'Now, why don't you move a little lower down my trunk so that I can drink you?'

'No. I don't think so,' said Raindrop. 'You are so very big and I am so small. I would not do just anything for your thirst. I'd like to have a little chat with you. I hear from the other animals that you can do absolutely anything you set your mind to. Is that right?'

'Of course it is,' said Elephant. 'There is nothing on the veldt that I cannot do. What do you want me to help you with?'

'Well,' said Raindrop. 'You know the big pan in the east. It is totally dry and all the animals around there are suffering very much. We, the raindrops are so very small and I don't think we will be able to fill the pan. Do you have any ideas?'

'That is not really such a big problem,' said Elephant. 'At least it may be a big problem for you, Raindrop, but not for a great animal like me!'

'So, what exactly do you propose?' asked Raindrop.

'Have you noticed how large I am?' asked Elephant.

'Yes, indeed,' replied Raindrop. 'I have always admired your magnificent size. Oh, if only I was as big as you! Then I would not have any problems filling up the pans.'

'Well,' said Elephant. 'Be that as it may. I cannot be bothered with your little problems. What I suggest is this. I will go and stand in the middle of the pan and have a pee. I am so large and I am sure that I will have no problems with filling up the pan.'

'Oh! Do you really think so?' asked Raindrop.

'Of course I do!' bragged Elephant. Just leave it to me.

'Oh! Thank you, Elephant!' cried raindrop. 'It is so very kind of you!'

So, Raindrop called all the other drops and they all moved away and it became sunny again.

The next day Elephant sauntered in the direction of the big pan. When he reached it, he went to the middle. Here he stood for a while and then he had a big pee. He looked down, expecting to see a lot of water, but there was nothing there. The pan was so dry that the urine had just soaked into the ground. So, he waited a while and then he had another pee and another and then, once more. But, still, when he looked down, there was not much to show for all his effort.

'Never mind,' he thought. 'The next time I meet Raindrop I will just tell him that I have completed the job successfully.'

A few days later, Elephant was standing in the veldt when the sun disappeared again behind a cloud and he felt Raindrop settling on his trunk.

'Hello there, Elephant!' cried Raindrop. 'Did you fill the pan for me?'

'Off course I did,' replied Elephant. 'I peed so much that I nearly drowned myself.'

'You are such a liar,' cried Raindrop. 'I have just been to the pan and it is completely empty. For such a large animal you are quite useless!'

'I bet you couldn't do better yourself!' grumbled Elephant. 'You are far too small to be of any use to anyone.'

'Then, come with me and I will show you,' said Raindrop.

So, they walked to the big pan and when they got there, Raindrop called all his little friends and they came together and they formed a massive cloud and it rained and rained and rained some more until the big pan was completely full.

Now, what do you think Elephant did? Nothing much. He just thought to himself: 'So what? If I tried a little harder, I could have filled this pan three times! Anyway, since all this water is here now, I may as well have a bath.'

So, he stood by the edge of the pan, filled his trunk with water and spouted it all over himself.

The raindrops watched all this and said: 'What a confounded, arrogant creature! He has no humility! He has no shame! He is wasting all that water! It should be for the animals to drink. Instead, he is using it to have a bath! I will teach him a lesson he'll never forget!'

Elephant was so busy with his cleaning that he did not realise that the clouds were getting thicker and thicker and that it was becoming darker. Quietly, the weather crept up behind him and shouted: 'Boooom! Booooom!' and at the same time, spouted a big, hot ball of lightning. It passed so close over Elephant's head that it scorched his ears. It hit the surface of the pan just in front of his trunk and it made the water boil.

If Elephant could, he would have jumped six feet in the air, but he was too big and clumsy. Instead, the shock shot one of his testicles up into his body, he was drained of all beautiful colours and became grey and wrinkled.

****

See the Afrikaners.

They have lived here for many years. They are a hardy race, who farm the land. Their origins were in Europe, but they have been rejected and betrayed by their past. So, now they have no fatherland, or motherland, or 'home abroad'.

Many years ago they were resettled in Africa and promptly forgotten by their European forefathers. So, now they are the 'white tribe of Africa'. This continent is all they have to call home. They have only the present to cling to. They have pledged their loyalty to this land and the land and the Afrikaners have a unique relationship: They are in mutual possession of each other, very much like an old, contented married couple.

They are a hospitable and most generous people. They are exceedingly set in their ways. Once they have pledged their loyalty, they will never take it away. Once they are settled, they do not like change of any kind. There are many of them who have lived here all their lives and who have never left the district, or the land.

See the Afrikaners

9. AFRIKANERS

I. FUNERAL

I remember when he died

And all the grown-ups cried,

Or, rather, how they tried

To perpetuate the lie

That he was a popular man.

And we, with heavy tread,

Paid homage to the dead.

In resignation bowed our heads

As we crowded round the bed

Of a very loathsome man.

'Come, children! Go and play!'

Our elders said. 'And, by the way.

'Don't enjoy yourselves too much,

'For your uncle Pete was such

'A very kindly man.'

So, they sent us on our way

And we ran towards the day,

While we left them there to pray.

And I heard my sister say:

'I hated Uncle Pete!"

While by the bed our elders,

Shedding copious tears

And, taking infinite care,

The body they prepared,

For the will had not been read.

With scents and soaps and oils

And water freshly boiled,

Like vultures at the spoils,

Unceasingly they toiled,

To gain entrance to his purse.

And while the grown-ups fussed

With fervent avarice,
I and Bess and Ross,
Behind the long-thorn bush,
Played marbles in the sand.

And when the corpse was dressed
And bathed and brushed and blessed,
Aunt Nellie said: 'Oh, yes!
'I really must confess!
'He was a handsome man!'

At last, with mournful gazes,
We donned our sombre laces,
To match our funeral faces.
And, vying for prime places,
We gathered round the grave.

'We're gathered here, dear friends,
'To mourn the tragic end
Of one of good intent,
'A truly worthy friend,
'A veritable saint.'

'A man above the rest,

'A rock. One of the best!'
But, silently, alas,
The vicar did confess,
The church-roof needed mending.

And when Oom Pete was laid
To rest among the glades,
Towards home our way we made,
Where all indulged in mead
And fares of quite the best.

Next day, his will was done.
Of riches there were none.
All speculated on
Just where his wealth had gone
And who had gained the lot.

Suffice to say, my father,
My granddad and his brother,
My dear, respected mother,
Agreed with all the others;
'A most atrocious man!'

II. LUNCH

They come in the middle of the morning. They arrive in two vehicles. There are eight of them; two adults and two youngsters in each car. To the woman, the old man and the children, the arrival of the visitors is an unexpected, but joyful surprise.

They all enter the house and settle themselves in the cool of the front veranda. Effortlessly, like the smoothest of engines, the tempo of the day increases. Within minutes life is re-arranged: Tea, biscuits and home-baked rusks are provided and instructions for lunch are passed on.

With inconspicuous stealth the children leave the room and the adults to their own company and talk. In aimless, easy companionship, they saunter through the orchard and make their way to the dam. On the way, they pick oranges which they knead with hands and fingers until they are soft and pliable. The skin is pierced and the juices and then the flesh are noisily devoured.

The morning passes in amiable companionship. Inside, the adults talk and outside the children play. And, so the morning progresses steadily. It makes its way towards midday where it turns the corner and moves effortlessly into noon and lunch.

The children are summoned from outside, the adults are roused from their comfortable seats and together they are herded into the cool of the dining room where they are seated at the big round table.

The door to the kitchen opens and a wagon-train of ladies appears. Each is laden with crockery, knives, forks, trays of food and, last but not least, containers of beer, ginger-beer and lemonade. The aroma of food fills the room; murmurs of appreciation are expressed by the seated assembly. The smacking of lips and drooling is quite audible.

When all is ready, eyes are closed, hands are held and the old man thanks the Good Lord 'for what we are about to receive'.

And so, to the feast. All tastes are catered for: Lamb stew, crispy roast chicken and baked potatoes, yams with crispy skin, pumpkin, green beans.

During the meal, various topics are discussed: 'Did you hear! Some lions got through Meneer de Graaf's boundary fence. So far they have killed four cows' and 'Oom Koos went for a weekend to Ngamiland. He says the flamingos are looking good this year'. For a pleasant while, things are mulled over, debated and, finally, exhausted and laid to rest for a slumber.

When lunch is done, plates, pots, pans and remnants of food are removed, whilst those round the table remain steadfastly seated. Beer is passed around; pipes are filled with aromatic tobacco and gradually, with the consumption of alcohol, conversation and laughter becomes more boisterous. The old man sheds some of his gentle, quiet demeanour.

After some time and beer has past, the woman taps her foot and he understands her disapproval in her action. Her tapping foot is saying to him: 'Don't you think you have had enough, Old Man?' He drains his mug and declines an offer for a refill. He is content with his lot.

And so, the afternoon passes. The children remove themselves to their outdoor entertainments and the adults settle in their comfortable chairs where they take pleasure in their conversations and their gentle familiarity with each other's thoughts.

Eventually the women remove themselves back to the veranda. Here they fall to lively chatter about their hopes, their pleasures, their little worries and their ailments. It becomes really quite competitive:

'When I have to do the ironing and I have to stand for a long time, I get this terrible pain in the lower region of my back.'

'I know what you mean,' says the second. 'When I sit at my sewing, not only do I have the pain in my lower back, but the discomfort radiates down the back of my leg as far as my knee.'

The third lady is not to be outdone:

'I was baking some cakes and bread and with all the bending, stretching, baking and kneading of dough, I also developed this pain in my back. By the evening, the ache went down as far as my ankle.'

And so, they spent the rest of the afternoon in most cheerful reminiscences of their ailments.

Imagine the time of day to be in the form of a statue, with the feet being dawn and the head as evening. Well, when the shoulders are approached, the guests prepare to take their leave. 'Do not wait so long before you come again', says the hosts and 'You must come and visit us next time', says the visitors.

The sound of the retreating vehicles slowly fades away on the still of the early evening air. At this time of year, the transition from day to dark is very swift and within a short while, gas-lamps are lit, suspended from the oak beams in the kitchen. It is here, at the table, next to the big old Aga, that the family unite to reminisce on the day that has been.

And so, eventually, the day comes to an end. It has been long and most eventful. A day in which friendships have been renewed and affirmed. But, most of all, it had been a day that was crowned by a magnificent lunch.

III. CHURCH

1

It is Sunday morning. The early morning farming duties have been completed. The old man, the woman and the child are seated at the kitchen table. They are having their breakfast, consisting of maize porridge and boerewors *26. When breakfast is finished, the old man leaves the house. He has to perform his regular chores, for the farm does not have a day of rest.

After the dishes are done, the woman and the child go into the lounge where they seat themselves on either side of the old valve radio. Its power supply is a large car battery. She twists the knob which turns it on, but they have to wait for some time for the valves to warm up and for the radio to respond. After some minutes the old wireless hisses and crackles into life and it is tuned to the Sunday church service.

For the next hour the audience of two listen to the service, the woman with devout attention and the child with his usual amount of confusion. The sermon is fairly standard. He has heard it so many times before. According to the parson, 'God is gentle, all-forgiving and benevolent'. However, if you should commit a sin, 'He will consign you to the eternal fires of hell, because he is a vengeful God'.

Another favourite story of sermons is the one about King David. He was in love with another man's wife. So, David sent this poor man in to the front line of a battle where he was sure to be killed. This is exactly what happened and the king took the unfortunate man's wife for himself.

Now, the Good Book says that David was 'The beloved of God' and there is no mention of him 'Burning in the fires of hell' after committing murder and the child had always believed that there was no more serious crime than depriving another of their life!

He had heard all this before and in the past; he had tried to discuss these things with the adults, but without much success.

'It is the will of God', or 'The vicar knows best. It will be foolish for us to question God or the parson'.

So he does his Sunday duty: He sits with the woman and supports her in her devotion. Eventually, his mind begins to wonder. He falls asleep.

2

It is Sunday. But, it is not any old Sunday. Today it is rather special. The parson is coming. He is making his quarterly visit to the district. All the families will join at one of the farms for church and lunch. Yesterday the old man, the woman and the child went to the shop to buy new clothes. The early morning passes swiftly in organised confusion of activity; breakfast, bathing and dressing for the coming event.

They arrive at the neighbouring farm in the late morning where they are enthusiastically greeted by a confusion of humans and animals. The elders seat themselves in the farmyard with cups of tea and scones, surrounded by three Rhodesian Ridgebacks *27, some turkeys and a variety of chickens, geese and Muscovy ducks. What an absolutely glorious assortment of life!

The youth are gathered in the shade of a tree in the front garden. Their idle chatter is gently enhanced by the responsible consumption of a few bottles of beer. After all, this is a holy day and the vicar will be arriving shortly.

At midday all is ready. They are gathered on the big veranda. The elders are seated on an assortment of benches and chairs. The youth are nonchalantly leaning against the walls or draped on the steps of the porch.

The grand sire of the community is seated at the organ, his feet placed in readiness on the treads of the bellows. He deserves a few words before we progress.

He is a silent man. When he is required to speak, his voice is quiet and rumbling, like a slumbering volcano. In the child's mind, he has always been old and silent.

The vicar greets the assembled and invites them to join in the first psalm: Psalm 23, The Lord Is My Shepherd. An old favourite. It is at this point that a most astonishing transformation takes place.

The volcano at the organ erupts. His feet stamp down on the bellows of the pump organ, his fingers pass over the keys with an unexpected dexterity and he leads the singing of the congregation and it is this which is the most remarkable. The voice that comes forth is loud, imposing, enthusiastic, all consuming. There is no hint of the normally quiet man.

The child is sitting in the corner of the veranda with his back against the wall. He follows the proceedings with detached interest. He has heard it all before: The all forgiving but vengeful God, the consequences of sins to the unrepentant sinner. Yes. He has heard it all before!

He leans his head against the wall. He falls asleep.

THE PRESENT

See the lodge

It is surrounded by the veldt. The rooms are spacious and cool. The green lawn stretches itself lazily and crawls down to the edge of the outdoor swimming-pool where it comes to rest and slumbers for the afternoon. A few tourists are seated in the shade of the scattered trees. The trees are trying their utmost not to sag in the heat of the midday sun. In the branches, the cicadas are hypnotically boisterous.

The tourists are watching a small dust-cloud in the distance. They are drinking cold beer and taking great delight in doing nothing.

The dust cloud gets bigger and, after a while, it brings with it a small pick-up truck which settles itself in the car park in front of the lodge. For a few minutes, the afternoon is transformed with some activity: A group of people alight from the truck, they unload some luggage and enter the lodge.

Then, all returns to normal: The lawn goes back to its slumbers, the tourists return to their beer and the cicadas continue with their croaky, monotonous songs. All is peaceful.

See the lodge.

10. LODGE

We leave the town and join the big tarred road. This road stretches for nearly one and a half thousand miles from Lobatse in the south to the northern border town of Kasane. After about thirty miles, we turn off on a dirt track and we reach the village, standing isolated, but bright and shiny on the edge of the veldt. There are no outskirts with solitary dwellings, standing guard, or acting as a beacon for the weary traveller, but we know we are close. The herds of cattle and tethered donkeys signify human presence. At first there is nothing but the snaking, sleepy, dusty road. And then, we are in its heart.

The single, cobbled street stretches lazily between the few houses and shops, past the borehole with its solar pump, its single solar panel gleaming brightly in the late afternoon sun. The sun also glares hot and fierce off the dust-clad buildings with their thatched roofs.

It is hot, too hot for any human activity. A lone dog crouches - in the shade of a mopane tree, staring at six scrawny chickens which are grubbing in the sparse grass. A fleeting thought of chicken-chase crosses its mind, but is soon scorched away by the midday heat.

At the village garage there is more activity. A young man is leaning against the door of his Toyota Landcruiser. He is talking on his cell phone. A young woman is cleaning the forecourt with a jet-washer. To the left of the garage, two solar panels collect the rays of the sun. On the other side of the panels stands a bungalow. On the roof of the bungalow a telephone aerial and a satellite dish proudly announce modern times and progress.

Then it is all behind us.

We travel through the afternoon, until we reach the evening and the lodge where we prepare ourselves for the magic of the night.

We sit around the camp-fire and stare silently into the red flames that flares with a redness which could only be the redness of fire, cloaked in the peaceful surround which could only be the peace of the veldt.

We listen to the silence of the solitary syringa and the dusk: The dusk which enfolds us in a blanket of serenity. We look across years of open space and stunted shrubs and grassland, at the sun, which is just about to fall off the edge of the earth.

We remember the past. We reminisce on our youth and the things we did. We remember those that have now long gone from us. We speak of nothing much and yet of everything that matters, for that which matters is not much and our silences say it all. We think of the day that was and the many miles we left behind and we relish with tired anticipation the coming of the night.

We hear the noises of the night: At first, the lone cricket, soon to be joined by its multilegged friends and, nearby, in the newly filled lake from the recent rain, an accompaniment of frogs and toads, all blending into a symphony of sound which is gentle on the ear.

We know them all.

My brother speaks with that many-miled-look in his eyes: 'Have I ever told you?' and he tells an unforgettable tale which will soon be beyond memory, because it will blend with so many other tales.

In the distance we hear the guardians of the night. The lion roars his disapproval: 'Wife! I am hungry! It is time for you to hunt!' The jackal gives a mournful cry and the hyena laughs. To the east, the wild-dogs yelp and the leopard, that crusty old gent, grunts them all to silence.

The night comes. With sudden stealth it throws a blanket over all. The brightly lit, pebble-dashed sky winks a salute to all Africa. The fire also now glows with the redness which could only be the redness of hardwood cinders.

My brother speaks and they all come to listen: The lion, the jackal, the hyena, the wild-dog and the eland and with them come the cheetah and the leopard.

The owl settles himself with a wing-sigh in the syringa. He says nothing, for he is wise and he knows that silence is the master of wisdom.

We listen.

My brother tells his many tales - Of droughts and dust, of heat and hunger and of the plenty that came with the rain, like an oasis in the barren years. He tells of those ancients and their gifts of paints and chalk: Those little ones, who are ancient of spirit even as they take their first breath. He tells of their gods: The sun and his wife, the moon, and their children, the stars.

We look at them and we believe.

He speaks with the lion, the leopard and the eland. They tell of their conflicts, but also of their respect for each other. For, though they are separate, they are bonded by the veldt.

We sleep, safely wrapped in the magic cloak of the African veldt.

POSTSCRIPT

I left Botswana for England in late 1968. All that I discuss and evaluate in part one of this book, concerns the people and the state of their lives during the fifties and sixties. I do not describe the lifestyles of the people of all Botswana. I am only concerned with the relatively small community of the district of Ghanzi, especially the white Afrikaner farmers and the Bushmen, since these were the folk I knew in my early years.

I was born and spent a large part of my childhood, on a cattle farm. From the age of seven until I was eighteen, I went to school in South Africa. I returned home twice a year: Six weeks over the Christmas period and three weeks in the winter. When I was eighteen, I left the African continent for England where I have remained. So, from the age of seven, I inevitably, by circumstances came to compare, evaluate and, ultimately, adopt some of the cultures and values of other countries. What I realised recently, was that there is a lot of truth in the saying: 'Familiarity breeds contempt'. Until I was eighteen, I took the life I led in Ghanzi for granted. I became bored with the quiet life and I was intoxicated and excited by life abroad. Not only do I feel regret for neglecting the values, cultures, space and precious quiet of this beautiful country, but I also feel ashamed of the fact that I was prepared to sacrifice and exchange my childhood values so cheaply.

What was here when I left? How did the people cope with day to day living? In what way are they better off now? Did they sacrifice some of their values for a modern lifestyle? These are some of the questions which I attempt to answer.

When I lived here in the district of Ghanzi, it was completely inhabited by cattle farmers. The farms were huge and largely devoid of modern facilities. For instance, very few of the farms had the luxury of electric power. In the house where I grew up, we used gas and oil lamps for lighting. A few farms had generators with which they could generate a small amount of electricity, but on the whole, all machinery and other equipment were petrol driven.

Even transport was of a very basic nature. For as long as I can remember, we relied for travelling to neighbouring farms on a little Ford pickup. One of the simplest, but equally, most exciting and pleasurable experiences of our youth, was to travel on the open back of the pickup, seated on empty oil-drums.

Sometimes it was even more basic. On the many occasions that we had trouble with the little truck, we travelled by horse and cart. Quite often, when work had to be done on the farm away from any roads, personnel and equipment were carried to the site on a wagon, towed by a team of donkeys.

Well, all that has changed now. Solar power enables many farms and most households to function with up-to-date, modern equipment. Instead of wood burning stoves, they have electric cookers; Instead of gas and oil lamps hanging from the beams, they have electric lighting; Instead of having to warm up water for washing or bathing on the Aga, they have electric hot water boilers.

Another thing which was closely linked to the lack of electricity was the non-existence of running water on the farm. If water was required, whether for drinking, or washing of people and clothes, it had to be collected from the windmills at the dams by bucket. This must have been a most tedious task, but since no-one knew any different, it was considered the norm and done without complaint.

Today, with the aid of solar panels and electric pumps at the boreholes, water can be pumped to all the places on the farm where it is required for drinking or washing. Water can also be pumped to the different cattle posts where electric pumps are installed to provide drinking water for the cattle.

One of the biggest changes is the modernisation of roads. When I was a child, all of the roads in Ghanzi, (and, I would safely say), in most of Botswana, were nothing more than dirt tracks. So, to visit neighbours, to do some shopping, or to travel either to South Africa or Namibia, was a major task. Consequently, visits to neighbouring farms were scarce and travelling to other countries was even more seldom undertaken. Botswana was a very poor country. But then, in the 1980's things changed and much for the better: The reason for this, was the discovery of diamonds. Since then Botswana became one of the fastest growing economies in Africa. Although there are still many dirt tracks on the farms, the major roads running across Botswana to the surrounding countries and from the north to the south across the length of the Kalahari, became wide and splendid tarred roads.

Many of the regular activities of the farms have also changed. For instance, on our farm we had cows specifically bred for milking. The cream was separated from the milk and stored in a cooler. Once a week the milk lorry would arrive and transport the cream to a town in Namibia where it was sold.

This activity has now been discontinued. The farmers rely totally on beef cattle for their living.

Something else which appears to have stopped in Ghanzi, is ploughing. On our farm, we produced corn and maze, mainly for our own consumption. One of the greatest pleasures of my childhood was to follow in the tracks of the donkey-drawn plough with my Bushman friend. There are certain things in this life which are beyond general explanation. Since ploughing and planting was done during the rainy season, the ploughed earth was slightly damp. Unless one experiences it personally, it is impossible to describe the beauty of the smell of slightly damp ploughed earth, the mixed scents of upturned roots and the feel of the damp earth between the toes of our bare feet. We loved it all!

Another major change in the last fifty years is in communications. When I was a kid, we had no telephones. Then, in my late teens, someone had the bright idea of creating a very basic 'phone system. It was achieved in the following way:

All the farms were protected by a grid of steel-wire fences. Inevitably, where neighbouring farms bordered on each other, the perimeter fences also joined together. So, someone had the grand idea of connecting phone cables from each farm to the top strand of the fences.

The phone apparatus was exceedingly basic. It consisted of a box, containing a dynamo, a handle to turn, to activate the dynamo and a hand-set.

It was really very simple to communicate with a neighbour: Just pick up the hand-set and turn the handle. An electric current was sent along the cable to the fence and from there to the other phones, causing them to ring.

A system of coding was introduced to indicate the person that was being called. For instance, two long rings and a short for Mr Le Roux and two long and two short rings for Mr van Dyck and so on. Inevitably, no-one took any notice of the codes and most of the time; everybody picked up their phones and listened in to each other's conversations.

Today that has all changed! All the farmers have cell phones. As a result of the vast distances between and on the farms, signal strengths are not always very good, but this is of little concern. There have been other technological advances. When I was a child, television was but a vague rumour. Our only means of communicating and receiving news from the outside world was through radio, but now everybody has a TV set. Most folk also have SatNav and computer systems. The result of all these technological advances is that the individual farmers are not as isolated from each other as they used to be.

Back then, the main industry was farming. Since then, a new occupation has arrived in Ghanzi: Safaris. This, inevitably, has led to some spin-off business developments, such as safari food supplies and a multitude of game-lodges.

The economic development of Botswana has also resulted in some changes in the towns. I remember Ghanzi as a typical one-horse town when I was a child. The single street was a dirt track. Now it has become a thriving town with a variety of supermarkets and shops, selling electronic goods, computers, clothes, and, the ultimate sign of prosperity, souvenir shops.

Have any of these new developments had a profound effect on the people of Ghanzi? I believe not. Since roads are vastly improved, visits to neighbouring countries are much more common, but very few of the indigenous folk of Ghanzi leave and settle abroad. This is their land and their people; A land where passing time is of no concern; A land where beliefs, whether religious, cultural, or lifestyle are seldom challenged; ultimately, a small space on earth where the land and the people can immerse themselves in a shared familiarity.

On their behalf, I would like to send a little prayer to their true gods, the sun, the moon and most of all, nature:

'Oh, Father Sun! Will you shine down on this land and all who live in it. Will you wrap them all in your protective warmth and keep them from harm. Mother Moon! Will you act as a guide to all at night, whether man, beast or ghost and will you fill them with peace. And, Nature! Will you caress the veldt with your breezes and, when you deem it right, will you gather your clouds and let the scent of rain fill the air. Amen.'

THE END

FOOTNOTES

1. Botswana: Republic of Botswana. A landlocked country located in Southern Africa.

2. Ghanzi: Ghanzi Town is in western Botswana. It is the administrative centre of Ghanzi district and also the capital of the Kalahari. The local language is Shekgalagari and the various local ethnic groups have a spirit of tolerance. The name Ghanzi derives from the Naro word "Gaentsii" meaning swollen buttocks. This may refer to the well-fed animals, collecting at the water-pans. Naro is one of the many Bushman languages of Ghanzi.

3. Kalahari: A large, semi-arid, sandy savannah, covering much of Botswana and parts of Namibia and South Africa. It is a semi-desert, with huge tracts of excellent grazing after good rains. The name, Kalahari, could well be derived from, Khalagari, meaning, 'A Waterless Place'.

4. Veldt or veld: The word 'veld' comes from the Afrikaans word for field. It is a wide open, flat area, covered in grass and shrub and occasional trees.

5. Bushmen: A nomadic people of Southern Africa.

6. Afrikaners: An ethnic group, descended from Dutch settlers and other ethnic groups living in Southern Africa. Their language is Afrikaans, which is primarily derived from 17th century Dutch.

7. Transvaal: An area of land north of the Vaal River in South Africa.

8. Voortrekkers:, Which literally means, "Those who pull ahead". The movement as a whole was known as, "The Great Trek". It means these were pioneers, or pioneer emigrants, who left the Cape Colony for the interior of South Africa in the 1830's and '40's.

9. Dorslanders: It means, 'thirst landers', because of the dry areas they moved to. These were a group of Afrikaners who left South Africa in the late 19th century. The majority settled in Namibia, but some of them crossed into Angola. Unfortunately the land here was very hostile and many crossed the border into Botswana where they attempted to settle at Maun. Many died here of malaria and they were once again forced to move. They went south from Maun and eventually settled in Ghanzi where they became a community of cattle farmers.

10Okavango Delta: A large, inland delta where the Okavango River ends. Much of the water evaporates here and is transpired by plants. It was declared the 1,000th World Heritage Site. 11Tswana: A Bantu, Southern African people. Their language is Tswana and they make up 80% of the people of Botswana.

12 Salt-pan: A salt-pan is formed where water evaporates, leaving minerals, usually salt. These minerals reflect the sun's rays and often appear as white areas.

13 Eland: The common eland is an antelope found on the Kalahari. It is native to Botswana. Its Latin name is *Taurotragus Orix*.

14 Gemsbok: Oryx Gazella. Native to the Kalahari.

15 Springbok: The springbok, (*Antidorcas Marsupialis*), is slender and long-necked. It is very common. It can run at speeds up to 62 miles per hour and it can leap up to a distance of 13 feet.

16 Bakkie: A pick-up truck.

17 Kappie: An old fashioned sun-bonnet, made of cotton and traditionally worn by Afrikaner, farming women.

18 Potjie kos: A stew, consisting of meat and layered vegetables, slowly cooked in a cast-iron, three-legged pot on an open fire.

19 Kraal: A fenced in area where the cows were rounded up for milking, or any other necessary functions, such as branding or vaccinations.

20 Stoep: An open veranda at the front of the house.

21 Wild cucumbers: *Cucumis Africanus*. Also known as gemsbok cucumbers. It is an oval, wild vegetable, which grows on a creeper. It is green with white thorns on its skin.

22 Steenbok: It resembles a small Oribi. It stands up to 62cm at its shoulders. It is a reddish, fawn colour. When it detects a predator, it will lie down initially and then try to escape by running on a zigzag route. They are known to take refuge in the burrows of aardvarks.

23 Duikers: A small antelope with small horns. They can be found in areas where there is sufficient vegetation for them to hide. Their name comes from the Dutch word, diver,

because they tend to dive into vegetation when they encounter a predator.

24 Indaba: A formal gathering where important matters are discussed.

25 San: Indigenous, traditional hunter-gatherer population of Botswana. San is another name for the Bushmen. There are many different groups with different languages. The San are one of 14 known extant 'ancestral population clusters', from which all known modern humans descended.

26 Boerewors: A traditional sausage, favoured by the Afrikaner community. It contains Coriander seed, black pepper, nutmeg, cloves and allspice. The meat is mainly beef, with some lamb or pork. Traditional boerewors is usually constructed as one, long spiral sausage.

27 Rhodesian Ridgebacks. These dogs were originally bred in Rhodesia, now Zimbabwe. They were also known as Van Rooyen's lion dog, or African lion hound. The Boer Hunting Dogs were a forerunner of the Rhodesian Ridgeback. It was valued as a hunting dog, because of its ability to keep a lion at bay so that its owner was able to kill it.

A Ghanzi cattle ranch

Rooibrakke, near Ghanzi

Some of the Lewis family members.

The 'old man' and his brotherwhen they were young..

Characters from Intermission, my parents.

Josef Lewies

Xgaiga Qhomatca, my childhood friend.

My mother's grave, at the family burial plot, below.

Giraffes approaching the waterhole at sunset.

From Rooibrakke Game Lodge, below.

The outskirts of Ghanzi town.

A Botswana sunset, Okavango Delta.